Rise of a Hero

Wind of Destiny, Volume Four

AJ Cooper

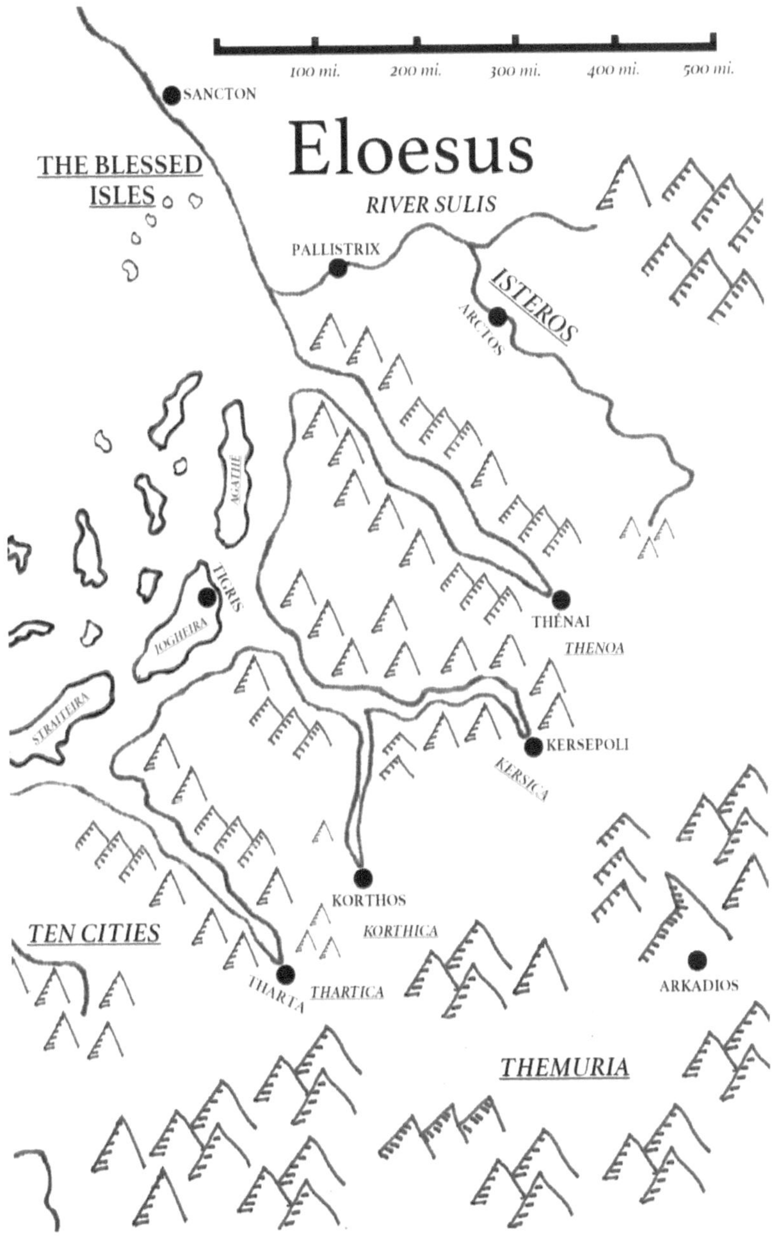
SANCTON
THE BLESSED ISLES
Eloesus
RIVER SULIS
PALLISTRIX
ISTEROS
ARCTOS
100 mi.
200 mi.
300 mi.
400 mi.
500 mi.
AGATHÉ
TIGRIS
IOGHEIRA
STRAITEIRA
THÉNAI
THENOA
KERSEPOLI
KERSICA
KORTHOS
KORTHICA
TEN CITIES
THARTA
THARTICA
ARKADIOS
THEMURIA

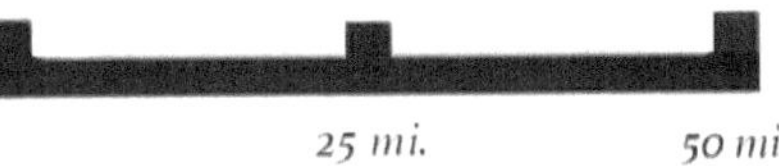

THE MIDDLE SEA

Khazidea

ONLY NOW

The women of Thénai—in olden times—were told to keep their hair covered and their mouths shut. They were to be neither seen nor heard—to remain shut-ins, to stay inside and never go out. Their homes were to be their entire world.

Pygmalia, a Thenoan woman of the highest pedigree, knew it was not olden times anymore. No woman covered her hair, nor kept her mouth shut. And a new god had entered the pantheon; a god more dear to women than Amara or Nix had reached Thénai from his home in the Arkadian hills. Brecko, lord of wine, invited all the desperate wives of Thénai into his nightly debauches.

Pygmalia had donned her leather mask; under the nose of her husband she had drunk an entire bottle of wine. She had half-walked, half-staggered outside into the streets of Thénai, and with her fellow Breckonals she had danced out of Lion's Gate into the cool of the outlying hills.

"Come ye Breckonals!" a voice shouted from the darkness. "Come ye, come ye! Come ye, Breckonals! Come ye, come ye!"

Pygmalia recognized that voice; her high priest had led her on this path before, up to new heights and to ever-greater states of ecstasy. The best Breckonals lost all inhibition and rational thought. To please Brecko was to become an animal, a creature and not a human being, a feeler and never a thinker. Pygmalia's best friend Demokrita—wife of a powerful demiarch—had achieved such a state of Breckonalia that she had lain with a hairy-legged satyr and cared not at all.

"Brecko!" Pygmalia cried. "Brecko!" She cared no longer, about no one, about nothing. This wine coursing through her veins, these thoughts, furious and unrestrained, this anger, this fear, this fury, this lust and passion, would rule her now and until the end of her days. "Brecko! Brecko!" she cried. Sweat dripped from her body as she ran to her high priest like a lamb to its shepherd. "Brecko! Brecko!"

A hundred women followed just behind her. They would tarry long from their husbands, for days. Nothing mattered, only this emotion, this passion—only this moment, not the future, not the past.

"Brecko! Brecko!" Pygmalia cried and her hundred sisters echoed her. "Brecko! Brecko! Come ye Breckonals! Come ye! Come ye!"

OUTSIDE THÉNAI

Theron was not a fool. He saw how people looked at him now. When Daphnë, the amazon queen, held his hand in hers, and they walked among Thénai's streets as man and wife, glaring faces greeted them. The citizens of Thénai spoke in bitter whispers among themselves. Theron's friends pulled him aside and repeated the insults and angry talk they had overheard. Theron's friends counseled him to leave Daphnë behind, to put her away and never speak of her again. But Theron did not listen to his friends. All the hate and angry talk inspired Theron to hold Daphnë even closer.

After all, she had sacrificed a lot. No longer was she queen of the amazons. She had put aside the throne for Theron's love. She had left her people. She had disembarked into Eloesus, onto this mysterious shore.

And then she had died.

A rare summer squall was drenching the golden grass when the grave was dug. Her body had been wrapped in linen sheets before being laid to rest in a coffin. There, they had set her with her most precious possessions—her glaive, her saber, her ten chakrams, her dagger.

Before the funeral, a priest had approached Theron.

"Do not be sad," he had said. "She is surely in the Fields of Paradise—"

"Enough," Theron had cut him short. He had not wanted any false encouragement of an imaginary afterlife. He had not wanted any kind words, any condolences.

He wanted only silence. He did not feel sad anymore—only cold and numb. Enough tragedies had been visited upon him. His heart had grown hard; he no longer cared about anything, or anyone.

He watched as Daphnë, his love, was laid down in the six-foot pit in Thénai's city cemetery, right outside Lion's Gate. How many friends had he lost? Phaido, Zoë, now Daphnë. He and Daphnë had talked of a life together; now that hope was gone, cruelly swept away. The gods were powerless; no longer did he pray. Before the gravediggers shoveled the first load of dirt, Theron left. He passed through Lion's Gate emotionless, unfeeling, cold.

CITY SQUARE, THÉNAI

When he reached City Square, questioning what it was that propelled him forward—what it was that caused his knees not to buckle, that caused his hands not to put a knife to his throat—he heard a loud voice calling from a lectern, brash and bold: "They have been robbing us!" the voice was saying. "They have taken our silver, our gold… they have contributed nothing!"

A fat man in a chiton stood there. His face was splotched red, wrinkled and distorted as he shouted.

Theron recalled that the election was only months away, that this was no doubt some citizen angling for a seat on Thénai's House of Assembly.

"We must answer their theft with force!" the would-be politician shouted. "We must not pay them a single *talon*! No, we must not pay anything. We should not rebuild their temple… we should raze it to the ground and leave not a single brick standing."

Was this man truly speaking against helping Korthos, which lay in ruins?

A crowd had gathered around him. He stood on the High Podium where government officials and visiting speakers made announcements.

"The Temple of All Gods has plentiful gold," he screamed. "If we raided the temple, we could erase our city's debts… we could have a prosperous future. If you vote for Kunar, I promise you that… a bright future, where Thénai is exalted. A bright future, where none question Thénai's glory. We will outshine Tharta."

Those gathered in the crowd cheered.

What a striking figure was this Kunar—fat and red-faced, shaking with fury. He was insane, but he was memorable. Among Thénai's well-educated and wealthy populace, he had no chance. But watching him quiver and twitch, watching his face turn a bright apple-red, attracted the attention of the crowd. Every eye was fixed on him, every ear attentive.

"We have given them so much!" shouted Kunar. "And for nothing in return!"

A gentle wind was blowing—well needed in this sticky summer heat. Theron thought of the war which had ended three years ago. Had it really been that long? He thought of Phillipidēs' arms and armor—Pyrax, and the Invulnerable Helm—which his fellow Eloesians had taken from him. He thought of the Oracle, the mad woman on the sacred mount. He thought of Daphnë and realized his life was passing away.

The old times had gone. Eloesus was proud and bolder than ever; each day, each week, each month more gold seemed to pour into the country's coffers, and it had all started three years ago, today.

THE FIELDS OF MARATHA, THREE YEARS AGO

The Fharese army had regrouped. In all their number, in all their hundreds of thousands, they had re-formed under the command of their dark captain, the one called Rogon. Rogon, a Rephathite—a giant standing six feet tall—had forced all these quarreling soldiers, representing a hundred bitterly-divided nations, into one cohesive force. It had been a task which even the now-dead King of Kings could not manage—yet it was a task that Rogon had completed.

Rogon's bulky iron armor was black as tar, and his helm's two winged spires resembled the antennae of an insect. He wielded a sword in one hand, which any man of lesser strength could scarcely hold in two. He heaved a great tower shield of shimmering metal in the other. His loyalty to the king had been unquestioned—until now.

~

It is not for him I fight, thought Rogon. *Not anymore.*

Rogon's loyalty to was his own name, to the land of Rephah, to the glory of Fharas.

The Eloesians had gathered to face them, numbering less than fifty-thousand. All the hoplites they could spare had locked shields in the Fields of Maratha. The waves of the sea batted against the shore and the air smelled of myrtle and coriander. It was here the final end of the Eloesians would take place. Their commander, Theron, had spoken with such arrogance. Rogon would make him eat his words... and then he would bind Theron to a stake, and burn him alive as a sacrifice to the gods.

CITY SQUARE, THÉNAI, PRESENT

Theron remembered that day clearly. Rogon, the so-called Dark Captain, had managed to wrangle together the Fharese remnant. They had outnumbered the Eloesians five-to-one. Rogon had met Theron personally, expecting terms of surrender. But Theron had laughed to his face, and refused.

What a memorable figure was that Rogon. His armor was blacker than any paint could color it; and his insectoid helmet made him seem twice as tall as Theron.

Of course, the day had not ended as Rogon expected.

The Eloesians—their morale buoyed by the King of Kings' death—had not only held firm against Rogon's onslaught, they had driven forward and broken the Fharese ranks. An inexplicable victory had been won that day, on the Fields of Maratha, and all doubts about Eloesus' victory against Fharas had been erased.

Celebrations had erupted in Thénai that night. Sacrifices of thanksgiving were made in the temples of Amara, Alabastros and Nix. A feast-day had been declared by Thénai's College of Priests. Hope and joy had burst forth: "*It is morning in Eloesus…*" said a poor beggar. "*It is a new age… we will never see trouble again*," Theron's friend had said.

Theron had commanded that very victory, on the Fields of Maratha. He had fought shoulder-to-shoulder with his brothers-in-arms. When the war was won, he had scoured the bodies of the enemy—and saw no black plated armor or insectoid helmet. Rogon had escaped.

~

A voice stirred Theron from his reminisce. "Theron." Unfortunately, he recognized the voice. He recognized its exact tone, he recognized its meaning—Hyron, Chief Demiarch, wanted something from him.

Hyron had not seemed to age at all in these past three years. Whereas when Theron looked in the mirror, he saw more gray hairs than brown, Hyron bounced through City Square in a carefree manner. The newfound wealth which was pouring into Thénai had erased the stresses of interest payments and fees for public works— Hyron no longer had to worry, and it showed.

"The Assembly needs you," said Hyron.

The nerve of this Hyron was something to behold. Theron had just returned from burying his love. At the thought of it, his eyes welled with tears. Who was he kidding? He was not cold and numb. His heart was not hard; he was as fragile as he had ever been. He wiped his eyes with his sleeve. "Leave me," he tried to say, but the words did not come. Only a croak left his lips.

"We have agreed to pay Korthos a ten-year, forty-*talent* loan," Hyron said.

"Oh, stop it," Theron wanted to say, but no words emerged. He was a shell of a man without Daphnë. He could not handle his duties as politarch, anymore. He would have to resign.

"You must see to the rebuilding of the temple and ensure each *thalon* is well used…"

Hyron did not understand what he was doing; he did not understand he was hurting Theron.

"You must ensure the loan will be repaid in full."

"I will," Theron said. There was no other way to distract from his pain.

~

It seemed every street was under construction. White pavestones were covering what had once been dirt. At every crossing, a colored plaza was being erected. Bronze statues of hoplites now flanked the gate to the Long Walls. As wealth poured into Thénai, each *orhos* was being spent on what Thenoans loved best: beauty, culture and art.

Even the dirt path within the Long Walls was under construction. Gravel was being laid and white pavestones—ordered from some far-off quarry—lay in piles as teams of workers dug with shovels. Theron dodged out of their way as they worked, their sweaty bodies glistening in the sun.

At last he reached the port. The docks were packed with merchants and ships idled by the harbor; there was not enough room. The Politarch of Public Works was making plans to enlarge the harbor, but the work could not come fast enough. The Archon of Thénai, Polykrito, had also said something of enlarging the port city itself, and doubling the width of the Long Walls. The demiarchs, however, had argued against it—saying that, if Thénai tripled the size of its library, "all other Eloesian cities would be forever put to shame."

Ahead, sailors were unloading vast quantities of amphorae onto oxcarts. The clay pots held olive oil, perhaps, or Thartan wine… anything to feed the vast and growing Thenoan populace. While Fharas was shrinking in the world stage, Eloesus was growing in boldness and strength.

Theron pushed his way through the crowds and dodged out of the way of a barrel-laden oxcart. The scent of spice was heavy in the air—so too were perfumes, concocted by the southrons and sold at outrageous prices.

"Make way! Make way!" A man on an oxcart was driving

away the crowd. "Eye-balm from the Blessed Isles! Black tunics, too. Come meet me in City Square!"

The future had never looked brighter for Thénai… but Theron had never despaired so deeply. In a matter of years, he had lost his best friend, Phaido, and his soon-to-be wife, Daphnë. The gods were dead.

~

An inn overlooked the seashore, *The Blue Triton*. Here Theron would wait for his ship. He would go to Korthos and try to forget. He would throw himself into his work to the exclusion of all else.

As he opened the door, the memory of Kunar the would-be archon stuck with him—red-faced and angry, shaking with rage—and he wondered if such a memorable figure deserved further thought.

THE HOUSE OF ASSEMBLY, THÉNAI

Hyron was growing too old and tired for these meetings. He thought more often than not of running away altogether, of abandoning Thénai's politics and becoming a laborer in some cobbler's shop. After all, his father had been a cobbler. Hyron knew how to cut soles, how to sow, how to bind leather shoes together.

"I ask that any demiarch with unspoken business would bring the matter before the Assembly." Hyron tried to sound enthusiastic, but undoubtedly failed.

Agathion stepped forward. Ah, yes, Agathion, who everyone spoke well of. *His wife is so well-behaved... his children are perfect.* Yet Agathion's dinner parties invariably involved dancers and prostitutes; and Agathion was a known pederast. "There is an urgent matter," said Agathion. "The women of this city have lost all shame..."

Hyron stifled a grin. Was Demokrita not as faithful and perfect as everyone believed?

"They have found a new cult to join," Agathion said. "Brecko the goat-footed god. From the Arkadian hills, his worship has been brought here, to Thénai, to the center of Eloesus!"

Brecko had no temples in Thénai. The pipe-playing "lord of the satyrs" was considered foreign; those who stooped so low as to worship him were forbidden from partaking in civic duties.

"The Breckonals, they call themselves!" cried Agathion. "They guzzle wine... bottle after bottle... and then they retreat to Arkadion and lie with satyrs. They must be punished... they must be stopped. We must issue a law against them."

The other demiarchs did not seem so concerned. One yawned. Another appeared to be sleeping.

"Unless there are objections," Hyron said, "I will call the Assembly to order; and we will all go home."

And then, like that, a demiarch stood up, Geon of Butchers Street. "There is a man trying for archon… his name is Kunar. The things he says are alarming… I am worried."

Several demiarchs chuckled—even Agathion. The matter Geon brought up, was, of course, no concern; but laughter was impolite. "Polykrito's term as archon has been popular! A madman named Kunar would never win the archonship anyway."

The demiarchs laughed even harder. Thénai's hundred-thousand citizens would never vote for a man named Kunar. Such a name marked him as a barbarian from Isteros. Thénai would not be led by an Isteroi. Thénai loved only its own. If—by some grand stroke of misfortune—Kunar had become a Thenoan citizen and offered a sacrifice to the civic gods, he would still never be a true part of society. This Kunar would be an eternal outsider—unloved by the city's people and the city's gods.

"I convene this Assembly," Hyron said. "Amara protect her city… Amara bless her city. Go in peace."

HEAVEN'S SQUARE, KORTHOS

This city owed Khloë.

With her sabers she had cut down seven southrons; with her hands she had pushed three more off the walls. Without the amazons, Korthos would never have survived; their city would be a burning heap.

And yet these Korthians glared at Khloë as she stood there. She was a citizen, now; she had paid her dues to the civic gods and been ceremonially welcomed into the Korthian community. So why did they still view her as an outsider?

She continued on through Heaven's Square. The temples lay in ruins. One's roof had collapsed; another's pillars had been knocked off by an amazon siege weapon. Was that why they hated Khloë? The mighty Juggernaut had destroyed their marble buildings and cracked the tile of Heaven's Square; but all that destruction had been for a purpose. The fiery stones which the Juggernaut had pelted upon Korthos had driven the southrons away.

Yet that was not why they hated Khloë; the cause of their grumbling and sneering looks ran deeper. She was a citizen but she was not one of them; throughout history none could join the Korthian family who was not born into it, but now Khloë, an amazon—*an amazon!*—could.

"Knife grinding!" a man said who had set up shop in Heaven's Square.

Sharpening her sabers was why Khloë had come to Heaven's Square. There was no war on the horizon, no battles imminent, but Khloë was an amazon, an amazon had to be prepared at all time for conflict. She tried to tell herself, "*I am not in Tigris anymore,*" but found herself walking toward the man anyway.

The man had set up a stone grinder which he had been pumping with his foot. "Two *thalon*."

The price couldn't get much lower; but Khloë had to wonder, judging by the slight scowl on the man's face, if there was one price for amazons and another for "true" Korthians. Nonetheless she dug the two tiny *thalon* from her coin pouch, and flipped them to the man. Then she handed him her sabers.

The man's eyes alighted as they saw them; they scanned the light, silver-colored metal, the black scrawl along its sides. "What is this writing?" he asked.

If only Khloë knew. "I bought it from a merchant ten years ago," she answered. "I don't know what the writing means… only that these are the finest sabers I've ever wielded."

What she said was not entirely true. The merchant—if that is what she was—had told her the meaning of the words: *"The one god is great, and we are at his mercy."* The woman had worn a gown of bright crimson, and her face had been so striking—pallid, yet with bright red lipstick. She had smelled of strange perfume. It was apparent she had come from a far-off land beyond amazonian knowledge; but Khloë had asked no further questions. Whatever strange culture the woman had come from, it was clear that she was cunning and manipulative—and if Khloë stared too deep into the abyss of her dark eyes, or listened too much to her cunning words, she would be drawn into a morass from which she could not escape.

The sabers were so sharp and fine, Khloë had no problem cutting down well-armored enemies. They were her most valued possession; if she had to choose between her Korthian citizenship and these sabers, there would be no hesitation in her decision.

The man began grinding the blades, sharpening them even as he eyed them with no small amount of covetousness.

"Have you heard, amazon," said the grinder as sparks flew from the sabers, "the news of Thénai?"

"No," answered Khloë. "And I am a Korthian, not just an amazon."

The grinder smiled mockingly. "Yes, yes, you are a Korthian. Our ever-wise archon Phaistion has surrendered to a city much less cultured than our own. He has signed a treaty with the damned Thenoans and accepted a loan from them… a loan that will be repaid by our children's children…"

Khloë did not understand the human tendency toward division and competition. It seemed—if left alone—every human culture would divide against itself.

"And that Theron is coming to oversee it all!" the grinder cried. "That amazon lover!"

Khloë glared at the grinder. The man Theron—the hero of the Southron War—had become well known across Eloesus. He had achieved such fame that Khloë knew instantly who the grinder meant. "That Theron," indeed. He was immensely popular with all the amazons of Korthos who had become citizens; it seemed Theron alone, hero of the Southron War, viewed amazons as valuable allies. Where Korthians turned up their noses at Khloë and her friends, Theron had intended to marry Queen Daphnë—yet word had spread of her untimely death. No doubt Theron was devastated. *Mira keep him,* Khloë prayed under her breath. *Mira bless him.*

Khloë would do whatever was necessary to support this Theron; he was a man set above, a man with a crown of destiny on his brow.

CITY SQUARE, THÉNAI

The plain red brick of City Square was being stripped away, revealing the pebbles below. The whole of the square would be redone in bright tile patterns of red, green, blue and white.

Hyron had wanted to spend the spoils of victory on practical things—an increase in salary for the army to encourage recruitment, a new fleet of warships, a trove of fine armaments for the hoplites—but as always, Thenoans had their minds on beauty and culture. The temple to Amara on the High City would be rebuilt, finer and gleaming white in color, and the forty-foot statue of the goddess within the temple would be outfitted in a gold-and-ruby cloak. The statue, Hyron's fellow demiarchs explained, would be crafted of ivory, with a cloak forged of gold. Moreover, the High City would be raised to a new height so as to dwarf all other cities forever. None would ever question the glory of Thénai then, nor would any other city "in this world or the next ever come close."

Already, Hyron had signed off on plans to double the number of parchments and scrolls in the city library. Could he do the same with these fanciful propositions to increase the height of the High City—and craft a statue built out of *ivory?*

Leave it to the Thenoans. Sometimes Hyron wondered if the always-serious Kersepolans had it right; no beauty, no adornments, just well-forged swords and mighty shields, bronze cuirasses and feather-plumed helms. Theirs was a practical people, a people not given to idle fancy. They had the greatest army in Eloesus, with every male citizen a great fighter—and yet, somehow, Thénai, city of artists and philosophers, had emerged the victor in this war. The overseas colonies—once under the thumb of Fharas—had, as soon as they broke free, pledged their alliance to the Thenoan League. From Palma in the desert to Lornadion in far-off Dys, from Bregantion in the north to Hyrkanos in the south, cities were pouring money into Thénai and swelling its ranks with soldiers.

Hyron laughed as he thought of the Kersican League. The cities who had pledged allegiance to Kersepoli were far fewer in number. Moreover, the Kersican League had shown signs of warming relations with the southrons. The Ten Cities had joined with the Kersican League, and brought with them a loyalist attitude to the King of Kings. To join the Kersican League was to betray one's people, to abandon Eloesus and join its enemies.

A voice was shouting above the sounds of hammers and shovels… a grating voice which seemed to squelch all others. Was this that Kunar whom everyone had been talking about?

Yes, a man was standing on the High Podium, fat and red-faced. His tunic was far too small for his immense body, and the buttons looked near bursting. His hair was sandy, with specks of silver. A large crowd, maybe two-hundred in number, had gathered around him—much more than the other hopefuls for archon.

Moreover, they were enthusiastic, cheering at his words; the current archon, Polykrito, had never roused people so.

"You hear my opponent Giton going on and on about the southrons!" Kunar howled. "You'd think he was mad, mentioning over and over again our victory!"

The crowd laughed. Hyron had done a small bit of research on this Kunar—he called it "our victory" but he himself was an Isteroi, from some small village. A commission had been set up by the Assembly to uncover whether he was a citizen and had determined Kunar became one only a year ago.

As a citizen, he could technically run for office; but why the blithe appeals to "love of Thénai" and "love of city" if he had lived here for a matter of months?

Kunar had earned his citizenship, however. Kunar, a wealthy landowner, had poured his considerable wealth into the Thenoan effort against Fharas—so much of his wealth, in fact, that the Politarch of Coin and Finance had recommended the granting of citizenship.

Before this Southron War, joining another city was almost impossible; now it seemed Eloesian governments offered citizenships wholesale, to whoever would pay for one.

Kunar's face twisted into a puckering, very unattractive caricature. "'Ah, we cannot forget the Southron War! Cannot forget it! Oh, we cannot lose sight of it! Cannot! Can-! Can-! Can-!'"

The crowd roared with laughter.

The election was a month from now, in the middle of summer; Polykrito was trying desperately to renew his three-year term. Signs of discontent were everywhere; and certain unscrupulous hopefuls were promising things Thénai could ill afford... "free bread" promised one Agemnon the Redhaired of Cobblers Street; "no more compulsive military service" promised one Naemos of Morgue Road. Little had been said of Kunar the Clown. The crowds of Kunar grew, but it was only because of the spectacle. Everyone loved watching a disaster.

"I'll tell you what we can't lose sight of!" Kunar howled. "The actions of this incompetent Polykrito! All this money, wasted on statues and roads and oh-so-lovely temples!" He lifted up a silver coin. "And he just minted these special coins. 'Liberty, 315!' Imagine the cost of minting these coins! Money that could be put to better use, I'd say!"

Watching from a distance, Hyron frowned. The crowd cheered at the words. The special coin, celebrating the victory in the Southron War, had been his idea. He had no idea it was unpopular... or was it? This Kunar knew how to rile people up. The money could be spent on other things... but on what? This

Kunar never said how he would spend Thénai's wealth.

Yet as he watched the red-faced Kunar turn once more toward defaming Korthos, Hyron promised himself that—unlike his fellow demiarchs—he would take the threat seriously. He would uncover Kunar's motivations, and do everything to thwart his archonship.

ALESIS, KORTHOS

The port town of Alesis was connected to Korthos in a similar way to Thénai: a pair of Long Walls which kept out pirates and robbers.

It almost felt like home.

But Theron had been feeling further and further from his home, even when he was in Thénai. It had changed; now the praise of the city officials had died down. Even the soldiers had begun to grumble—having forgotten the lessons of the Southron War—of Theron's "love for amazons." The threat was gone; now Eloesians had the opportunity to do what they loved best—fighting with each other.

He stepped off the deck of *The Siren's Call.*

A woman stood on the dock, old and decrepit. She was shouting. "Here he is! The one who brought the amazons to our shores… The one responsible! Who brought the amazons! Who destroyed the temple of our mother Nix!"

She had covered her old face with silver powder. A silver figurine of an owl was in her right hand, a figurine of a dog in her left—both symbols of Nix, Queen of Sorcery.

Hurt, Theron stepped back. He did not know whether he wanted to wring this woman's neck, or go hurl himself off the ship and have the waves take him. He had lost Daphnë his love; he had lost Pyrax and the Invulnerable Helm, the sacred armaments of Phillipidēs. He had lost the respect of his countrymen, who so quickly forgot the lessons of the Southron War. What else was there for him in this world? He had begun to fray at the seams.

Theron snarled and charged ahead, shoving the woman to the ground.

"A curse! A curse I proclaim!" howled the woman as Theron left. "May your eyes be pecked by screech owls… your heart pierced by a silvered sword…"

~

Heaven's Square was indeed a ruin. The amazon bombardment had knocked away pillars and caved in roofs. The cost of rebuilding would prove monumental; perhaps discarding the debris and starting anew was the best option.

The archon of Korthos met him in Heaven's Square, in the shadow of the High City. There, on the lofty mount, the once-pristine Temple of Arephon had caved in; it was not a building anymore but a pile of broken pillars and scattered masonry. *Perhaps these angry crowds have a point,* thought Theron. *Did the amazons really need to aim their Juggernaut at the High City? Did they really need to cause so much destruction?*

"Here he comes," said the archon, beaming. Several dozen hoplites in green capes and green-crested helms stood behind him, bearing shield and spear. "Theron, the hero of the Southron War." He bowed. "Phaistion. A pleasure to meet me, I am sure."

Theron could not bring himself to smile. "Thénai has promised forty *talents*. The loan must be paid in full within ten years."

"So I have gathered," said Phaistion. "Moreover we will be added to the Thenoan League at no cost… our name in the registry, our city protected. A great deal, it is said; one that cannot be missed. Come with me, Theron, to the High City. We will put it all in ink."

~

The High City of Korthos seemed to overlook the world.

Without the immense Temple of Arephon blocking the view, the High City seemed to skirt the clouds; and everything in this world and the next could be seen from its lofty height.

Like Thénai, Korthos had its law courts on the High City; even now a judge sat at his bench and a criminal was pleading before him.

It became apparent a group awaited them; a few dozen red-caped hoplites with red crests on their helmets.

Before Theron could turn and run, the hoplites behind him had pinned him to the ground and were tying his wrists together with coarse rope.

"Ah, you are so naïve, Theron," Phaistion said. "To think Korthos would stoop so low as to submit to Thénai… to join a league with an inferior city. A hundred times a hundred *talents* isn't worth it. We have thrown our lot in with Kersepoli. We have joined the Kersican League. And we are seizing your money."

Only two *talents* sat in the hull of the ship, in mixed gold and silver coins. Surely Phaistion knew that.

"You will fetch a nice ransom, 'hero,'" said Phaistion. "And then, when every last *doukos* is paid, your city will fall."

'THE DANCING SATYR,' CITY SQUARE, THÉNAI

In a tavern called *The Dancing Satyr,* overlooking City Square, Hyron poured a glass of fine Arctian red... a drink he hoped this Isteroi would like.

Where Kunar had shaved his beard and wore his hair in Thenoan style, this man, Kunar's friend Tyrosion had no shame about his Isteroi heritage. Tyrosion's hair, a shade of dark brown, was wild and matted, showing none of the care or oilings common among Eloesians. His bushy beard was thick and long, drooping halfway down his chest. Though he had lived for months among the citizens of Thénai, it seemed he had not availed himself of a bath or purchased any perfume; even now fleas were buzzing about his head, and he stank of sweat and grime. He showed no sign of caring what Thenoans thought.

Tyrosion eyed the goblet suspiciously. It was crafted of glass, with floral patterns painted along its edge. People told Hyron that the Isteroi drank their wine in plain leaden cups or even clay bowls. He had thought it rumor; perhaps it was true.

"I don't drink wine," said Tyrosion.

Hyron knew a liar when he saw one. This Tyrosion did not trust him. Fair enough; it made sense. Hyron and the demiarchs were adamantly opposed to his friend's archonship; would it be out of character to slip poison in the drink? "My Tyrosion," said Hyron, "I don't understand your friend's eagerness to become an archon... of a city he is barely a part of."

"There is little for him in Chorenē."

Chorenē, the tiny farming village in Isteros from which this problem sprang, was unknown to practically everybody. Yet Hyron had done his research, learning that no more than a hundred souls lived in Chorenē and that the only source of wealth was the surrounding vineyards.

Yet somehow, the pompous, blustering Kunar had been produced there, in that nondescript village. Somehow tiny Chorenē had given the great city of Thénai a serious problem.

"You do not trust me," said Hyron. "But perhaps, if you tell me what Kunar is after, you can profit from it…"

Tyrosion sneered. "An Isteroi does not take bribes."

Hyron sighed. This Tyrosion would crack, one way or another, but he had not found out how yet. "Out of the goodness of his heart, will an Isteroi tell a concerned citizen?"

"An Isteroi has no goodness in his heart," Tyrosion said. "The mothers of Isteros make sure of it."

Wild Isteros. Hyron sneered. They were warlike, the lot of them. They were Kersepolans without the culture. They had no traditions of politics or the finer arts. Even their capital, Arctos, was a tiny village in comparison to Thénai. *I cannot let my arrogance show.* Parry, strike, feint. *A politician is like a swordsman on the field of battle –* so he had been taught as a young protégé. Parry – defend against another's words. Strike – attack your enemy's character. Feint – stretch the truth when it benefits you.

"You are so loyal to a man who speaks ill of you," said Hyron. *Feint.*

"Speaks ill of me," repeated Tyrosion.

"He comes to the Assembly often," lied Hyron. *A greater feint.* "All would-be archons do."

"And he speaks ill of me," said Tyrosion.

"He speaks ill of Chorenians in general," said Hyron. "Not just you."

Tyrosion glared. "Chorenians are drunkards. And Kunar greatly profits from their drunkenness."

Hyron examined Tyrosion. What were his weaknesses?

Were there ways of finding them?

"I know you are a liar," Tyrosion said. "Everything you demiarchs and politarchs and archons say has some ring of falsehood. I am Kunar's best friend and dearest protector. He has never been to the House of Assembly, not once. You have never invited him. You have not taken him seriously, he thought—but now I know the truth. You are afraid."

Gooseflesh tore across Hyron's skin, and the room seemed to turn as cold as a winter's wind. There was no way to *feint*, to *parry*, to *strike*. It dawned on Hyron that, somehow, Kunar—untrustworthy and erratic—was going to win the election; and whatever motivations he had, the Assembly would not find out before it was too late.

HUDOR'S PRISON, ALESIS, KORTHOS

The cell was dank and cold, despite the hot summer. The rope had been tied so tight around Theron's wrists that they cut into his skin. A gag had been stuffed in his mouth, and a blindfold had blocked all vision before his sweat caused it to fall away. Now he could see the bare stone, wet from a recent rain; the roof still dripping, the floor slick with scat and piss. Thousands of prisoners had been held in this cell, and none cared about their wellbeing enough to clean.

The food, it seemed, was designed to torture—stale bread with a film of mold, a cup of murky water in a leaden glass, and withered grapes. The Thenoans would pay any ransom to see him freed, surely—but Theron had a nagging doubt, a feeling he would spend countless months in this prison before he finally took ill and died.

The door to the cell swung open and the guard swaggered in. "On your feet!"

Theron tried to stand, but his ankles were bound together. He slipped on the grime of the cell floor. He hit the hard stone and the guard began to laugh. He walked over, yanked Theron by the hand, and dragged him into the torch-lit hall.

Through the stone corridors Theron was dragged, until his rope-cut ankles began to bleed. In a pool of filth amid the prison walls, he caught sight of his reflection—and saw a man pale and thin, sickly and malnourished. The man he saw was just barely clinging to life, mere steps from the grave.

His body was bruised and dragged across chipped, uneven

floors, but soon enough the journey ended.

The light blinded him; a window with shutters open overlooked the sea. The sun's brightness was almost unwelcome after Theron had become a creature of dark caverns.

The archon of Korthos stood there, smiling; together with a woman in robes of gold. And there was one standing there he did not expect, one he did not believe he'd ever see in his lifetime.

He recognized the armor, black as tar; the pauldrons, red as blood; the bulky legplates and breastplate and sabatons. He recognized the helm, with antennae like an insect; and the towering height of its bearer.

Here was Rogon, the one whom Theron defeated at the Fields of Maratha. Theron had defeated him, man to man; and yet he dared show his face.

His tower shield was strapped to his back and his giant sword was sheathed at his side. From the helm's visor stared eyes like black coals.

"Traitors," Theron breathed.

The woman in the gold robe laughed. Her hair was auburn, her eyes green. "Traitor, a funny word. One that has no poignancy to a person of intellect. You may have won a battle, Theron, but look at you now... tied up and weak, starving and pale."

"I won a battle *for you*." Theron's voice had lost its strength; it was hoarse and wheezing.

"You won a battle for no one but yourself," the woman said.

"Enough, Gaia," boomed Rogon. His Fharese accent was difficult to understand. "This man is worthy of respect. He lost the war, but he won a battle."

Theron laughed. "I won the war, Rogon. You merely

captured me unawares, when I was trying to do a good work. You got the dregs of Eloesus to trick me… the very scum of the earth.”

Gaia smiled. “You are at our mercy… I suggest you choose your words carefully.”

“I am at no one’s mercy,” said Theron, “except my own, and the holy gods.”

Gaia laughed. “Indeed.”

“Why have you brought me out here?” asked Theron. “To show me Rogon… to show the depths to which you have descended? I wonder if the citizens of Korthos know you have joined league with the Fharese…”

“The citizens of Korthos despise you,” said the archon Phaistion. “Cheers were heard all around when they’d heard what we’d done. And as to why we’ve brought you out… we want you to glimpse freedom. You can taste freedom again if you provide us with what we need.”

Theron would not provide them with anything, especially if they needed it.

“You once had in your possession an ancient artifact… an engine of war of the Old Dominion. Some say it can vaporize entire cities.”

Theron had heard of the mechanism, a giant machine. The cluster of cogs and wheels was called the Hymnos Device after the island where it was found. It had been covered in corals and barnacles, but expert artisans had picked it apart until a clean metal machine was revealed. The vast machine, six feet by five feet in length, only whirred to life when the lock was decoded:

⌐ ⊣ ⊣ ⊣ ⊣

The esoteric code only caused sputtering and sparks. Yet experts on Old Dominion artifacts testified to the Assembly that this was one half of a fully-functioning war engine which—when given proper fuel—could blast walls and buildings to dust.

The Assembly had sent out an expedition to the Blessed Isles to uncover the second half of the Hymnos Device. Yet the other half had never been recovered. The salt waters of the Middle Sea had produced nothing. Surely it lay somewhere, buried underneath the sandy shoals.

"I do not know what you mean," lied Theron.

"Under your nose, we stole your beloved Hymnos Device," said Phaistion. "And you were privileged with the code. We know this by our spies. Tell us, Theron."

"I don't know anything about the Hymnos Device... certainly not the codes."

"He lies," said Gaia.

Judging by the way Phaistion glanced back at her and her bold glare, her crossed arms and hands, Theron had come to think Gaia was the true power behind the Korthian government—dominating both the archon and Rogon.

"Korthos is too enlightened to use torture," said Gaia. "Torture is the mark of inferior cities and barbarian cultures... but we will break you nonetheless."

"You will not break me," answered Theron, "not even with torture."

"Before the inventor Agenor died," said Gaia, "he made a design... a copy of the vast Old Dominion war engines. Without this other half we could never have pieced everything together. But now we can... and soon enough, the Thenoan League will be done-for."

Code-breakers had learned after many botched attempts that—with enough failure at the lock—the Hymnos Device would self-destruct. The self-destruction mechanism had been disabled. If only the Thenoan Assembly had the foresight to destroy the device altogether, there would be no threat, no Korthian theft, nothing.

A wiser man than Theron once said, "If you find a machine covered in barnacles and sea foam, bury it twenty feet underground and never speak of it again." He'd never heard anything good coming from Old Dominion mechanisms.

"Take him back to his cell," said Gaia, "until he rethinks his ways."

~

And into the cell Theron went. That night he ate moldy bread and an apple core. He washed the meager fare down with befouled water and cursed the wreck his life had become.

HEAVEN'S SQUARE, KORTHOS

It was days like this that Khloë remembered how much she had left behind.

A young man had popped the cork off a bottle of wine and taken a deep swig. News had spread of Theron's capture—Theron, "the amazon lover." "I hope he dies in prison!" he shouted to his friend. "Slowly!"

These Korthians had discarded Theron, a good citizen, like refuse. They had poured scorn on a hero who had rallied the people during the Southron War.

Khloë remembered her life in the Amazon Isles. Like everywhere, it had its challenges. The queen's absolute rule gave little regard for the common tailor or shepherdess. The burning sun—which they worshiped—sometimes brought famine to the land. But a hero such as Theron they would hold in high regard, second to the holy gods.

When she swore the vows of citizenship and made an offering to the civic gods, becoming a part of the Korthian community, she had left behind her sisters, her mother, her house, her beloved cats, even her amazonian identity. The amazons would not take her back; in their eyes she was little better than a traitor.

And now—having foresworn everything she had ever known, having given up her old identity—she had never felt more alone.

If these native Korthians included her in a conversation, her outsider status was clear. Her name is in the Registry of Citizens, but she will never be a Korthian... she is an amazon. Her leather armor, her sabers, her confident gait, her battle-readiness, her physical and emotional strength—these all set her apart as an outsider. She could never be one of them.

Quietly Khloë made her way down the square. She had come to purchase raisins, some flour perhaps, a jar of oil, maybe even a bottle of wine.

But remembering that young man's voice, his arrogance, his scorn, his glee at Theron's misfortune—a rage was building inside of her.

Khloë's rage surprised her. She had learned that it would build up for years without her knowing until… in one dreadful moment… it released in a burst of violence.

One night in her youth she had struck her mother, after witnessing—for years—the beatings and insults directed to her father.

It was like that, now, that fury… but what could she do? She would lose her citizenship if she tried to break him free from prison. And then what would she have left? Where would she belong? She had given up her amazonian identity; she had sprinkled oil and wine on the altars of the civic gods.

But I have to do something.

Someone was shouting: "Come one, come all… the Academy will teach you what you need to know."

A man stood there in a white chiton. Khloë had seen him in Heaven's Square before.

Philosophers had gathered in an olive grove. The Academy, they called this gathering. The greatest of the philosophers would teach the young and impressionable among the shady olive trees. Tests would be given—tests of memorization and logic—and if, years later, they proved their worth, these younglings would be given a scroll, signifying their accomplishments. Silver and gold was poured into the philosophers' coffers—all for a slip of paper, a diploma.

"Come one, come all… Korthian and Thenoan…

barbarian and Eloesian… amazon and human. Come seek the knowledge you so desperately need."

The amazons placed little value on learning, and even less on philosophy. Exhaustive conversations on morality and "the best possible good" was considered an utter waste of time. The swings and jabs of the glaive, the best and most lethal techniques with the saber, the deadliest way of hurling the chakram and javelin—those were the only topics worthy of study. And yet this philosopher had explicitly invited amazons. Khloë found herself walking up to him. Against all she had been taught, against all she had been trained to do, she found herself seeking the advice of this foolish philosopher with his head in the clouds.

The philosopher in the white chiton smiled. "One thalos for your first lesson, my good woman."

Khloë fished a small thalos out of her coin purse. The least valuable coin, it still would have seemed too much to part with just an hour ago—yet now she sought the advice of this stupid fop.

~

The olive tree was ubiquitous across the amazon world and Eloesus, but the Eloesians seemed to have an almost religious reverence for it. This grove, located in the middle of the city, had olive trees planted in exact rows. The branches were trimmed and kept healthy. The fruit had begun to grow, but wouldn't be ripe until the autumn.

The philosopher in Heaven's Square, Khloë learned, was named Nikon. "I got my diploma just last year," he had told her. "Now I am a junior teacher."

Nikon had written a book about why all cities should be ruled by kings, and why democracy was an abomination. The more he talked, the more Khloë had questioned why she had wasted that precious thalos. She could have bought a loaf of bread or a glass of wine. And yet others had joined her in her folly… a man who looked too old to walk the streets without a cane, even an expectant mother. They had paid their thalon, all to hear this mad philosopher talk.

The students took their seats among the mixed grass and dirt between the olive trees. Khloë, ashamed to even be there, took her seat last. Nikon loomed above them. His hair was long and a youthful beard had begun to grow across his face. His white chiton showed signs of wear, and was splotched with dirt. Yet somehow, Khloë, an accomplished warrior, had stooped so low as to seek his advice—and not only seek advice, but pay for it.

"Live long enough," said Nikon, "and you will see the world is an illusion. Live long enough, and you will see your true insignificance. Very few make their mark on this world… very few alter destiny. If you realize you are insignificant, you will see your troubles do not really matter. You will see that—when this illusion called life ends, and you return to dust—all the things that pain you, all the things that cause you turmoil, have no meaning."

Amazons taught that some people did truly change the world… some people had destiny "hovering about them like a crown of light." But amazon sages also said every life was significant, every life helped weave the threads of destiny, and that when a thread was broken, the gods wept.

Khloë stood up. Nikon was staring at her, aghast.

Theron had a part to play in this world. Even if it meant exile, even if it meant belonging nowhere, she would rescue him. Theron, savior of the amazon people, hero of the Southron War, lay in jail, hungry and suffering. If the wicked Korthian government slew him, a great thread of destiny would be broken.

Khloë fled the olive grove, promising herself she would fight. She would fight with everything in her. She would rescue

Theron, and preserve his place in destiny.

THE HOUSE OF ASSEMBLY, THÉNAI

Weeks Later…

Hyron bit back a snarl.

With the election just a week away and nerves high—and with the news of Korthos' betrayal public knowledge—the ambassador dared show her face. Her striking green eyes had a haughty look to them. Her arms were crossed and a smirk was on her face. Her robes—sewn of gold cloth—would easily fetch three-hundred *doukon*. Her bracelets were of white gold, inset with rubies that sparkled in the sunlight. This was a woman of means. She called herself Gaia.

"You promised us forty *talents*. There were only two on board…"

Hyron sneered. "And you availed yourself of them. It takes great courage to show your face, now."

"We have your hero Theron in Hudor's Prison."

Hyron gasped. Korthos went to great lengths to show its high-mindedness and charity, but Hudor's Prison was a black mark on their conscience. They had been known to leave prisoners there, in binds and shackles, and let them starve. Korthian citizens almost never went to prison; but those the Korthians considered less than they could expect harsh treatment and damp, disease-prone conditions.

"Some say he is Amara's own son." Gaia smiled. "But somehow, I doubt the goddess will rescue her child. Already he has grown gravely ill. I expect him to die within a fortnight. I will release him to you if you pay the remainder of the forty *talents*. He will be on the next ship from Korthos."

Shouting erupted from every corner of the Assembly House… demiarchs were cursing and sneering. Gaia seemed to enjoy it; her smirk turned to a beaming smile. She did not seem to realize the precariousness of her situation; she had brought with her five-hundred hoplites and fifty horsemen, but Thénai could easily crush them and bind her in shackles. *Yet she knows we won't. That is why she is smiling. She knows we won't risk a war.*

"Silence!" cried Hyron, and for once the two-hundred bickering men, young and old, stopped their shouting. For once, they obeyed Hyron, the rightful leader of the Assembly. "You are bold, Gaia! I assure you… one day, we will wipe that wretched smile off your face."

Her smile only seemed to grow. "We demand thirty-eight *talents*, paid in gold. Otherwise, your hero will die."

"The hero who saved you," Hyron said, "who stopped Korthos' imminent destruction. This is how you reward him… with shackles and chains." Yet Theron, "that amazon lover" had grown unpopular even in Thénai. The Southron War was now a mere memory, and a generation was growing up who would forget it entirely.

"You are not getting a single *thalos* from the treasury," Hyron said. "I would choose your steps wisely… you may find yourself soon at war."

Thirty-eight *talents* would have strained city finances just five years ago, but the spoils of victory had made it a small sum in comparison. It was the principle of the thing. And besides, very few in the city cared that Theron was in prison.

"I object!" shouted a voice. The archon Polykrito emerged from the shadows of the Assembly House. "I overrule this House's decree. The city may have forgotten Theron's heroism, but I have not. He is the one who united us. He is the one responsible for our victory in the Southron War.

"This witch will have her thirty-eight *talents*. Compared to Theron's life, that is a small sum."

Gaia smiled brighter than before. "My ship is waiting in the dock…"

HUDOR'S PRISON, ALESIS, KORTHOS

Six Days Later...

In Thénai, condemned murderers and rabble-rousers were fed bowls of hemlock. Within minutes, you would grow cold and begin to sweat profusely. Horrible pains and aches would set your stomach alight. At last, as the poison worked its way through your veins, you would cry out and gasp, unable to breathe; and hours later the prison warden would find you curled up on the floor, with vomit and foam trickling from your mouth.

As horrible as it was, Theron preferred a bowl full of hemlock to this torture. He could not hold down the moldy bread and putrid water. Even starving, he had to eat his food one tiny bite at a time, or he'd throw up over his already-soiled prison cell. The befouled water was perhaps responsible for his fever. At night, in cold sweats, all he had was a thin cot to keep himself warm. His clothes had been torn to rags by the torture. With prongs and searing-hot brands, they tried to break him; they tried to force the code out of him. They knew the value of the Hymnos Device. Like all engines of war designed by the Old Dominion, its destructive power was without question.

Yet despite all the torture, he had kept silent. The Korthians wouldn't pry anything out of him. If they pulled out his tongue and ripped out his fingernails, still Theron would not say a word. Pain he could endure; but disgrace he could not.

He had long come to realize that Rogon—the hulking giant in the black insect armor—was bedding this Gaia. He had also realized that Gaia—Korthos' chief ambassador—was a married woman. The effort to break Theron and destroy the Thenoan

League was being led by an adulteress. A female archon was not entirely unthinkable, and surely she had her eyes on the position.

For some reason, locked alone in this prison cell, he had begun to remember the striking face of Kunar. His sandy-blonde hair, his portly physique, his clenched fist hitting the lectern as he ranted and raved—all those things were burned into his memory. Somehow he had become convinced that this Kunar would win the election, and become Archon of Thénai.

The door opened, revealing the form of Gaia. The silhouette of Rogon—like a giant black bug—lay just beyond the threshold. Smiling as always, Gaia said, "Your city has abandoned you."

He knew the words were true, he knew it beyond all doubt.

"Your Assembly has refused to pay your ransom. And you refuse to give us the code…"

Theron's heart sank at the deep betrayal. Gaia's lies were profuse, but Theron could sense the hatred of his fellow Thenoans. On this matter, she spoke the truth.

"Thus a beheading has been scheduled… publicly, in Heaven's Square. Seven days from now, at midday." Gaia turned to leave.

Alone in the dark, Theron wept. He had lost Daphnë. Now he had lost his city. There was nothing left for him, nothing but death.

CITY SQUARE, THÉNAI

One Day Later…

Election day. Hyron walked through the square alone.

The Assembly still refused to believe there would be a change in governance. Polykrito had done well as archon; the treasury overflowed and the city was growing more beautiful by the day.

"Amikron is a dumb bore, fat and old—no one will vote for him," the demiarch Acromedē had said.

"Theomedion is stupid! He won't get more than a dozen votes," another had said.

And as for Kunar—when Hyron raised the alarm—the Assembly burst into laughter. The fat, doddering fool who was not even a Thenoan could not possibly win.

Yet Hyron believed they severely misread the mood of the people. There was angst… there was anger, directed at all corners, but especially at the Assembly itself. The ransom, paid to Gaia, had not helped.

Just yesterday, in the square, Hyron had heard a man shouting: "We paid those Korthians a fortune! And for an amazon lover."

Indeed, he had seen protests in city square—wild mobs chanting "Death to the demiarchs! Death to the demiarchs!" One group had laid hold of the demiarch Ason and demanded a city-wide vote.

"I have paid my taxes diligently!" he had screamed. "And you are spending it on that amazon lover! I'll have your head cut off! We're going to elect Kunar!"

In City Square, there was a High Podium and a lectern on which government announcements were delivered. But anyone could take the High Podium who ran for office.

And it seemed every day, Kunar spoke to a larger and larger crowd. The breadth of his support grew by the day. Just last evening, he had gathered before a mass of five-thousand, shouting, "We will bring these soft-bellied demiarchs to justice! These scoundrels, who paid a ransom for an amazon lover!"

The crowd had cheered, last evening, breaking into a chant, "Kunar! Kunar! Kunar!"

Hyron—watching from the shadows—had felt a distinct chill worm its way up his spine.

~

Hyron spent the rest of the hot summer day pacing the square. He was waiting for fate to reveal itself, for the path of destiny to be shown. He feared above all else Kunar—Kunar, the outsider, who was not even a Thenoan, whose motivations were inscrutable.

As the sun's power began to fade and a cool wind blew, Hyron—a self-avowed skeptic—decided to do what only common people resorted to in times of trouble. From a vendor in City Square, he purchased a morning dove. Then, cage in hand, he made his way up the steep steps to the High City, to the sacred temple of holy Amara.

~

Exhausted, Hyron paused. Sweating and panting, he rested his bones briefly, sitting on a stone seat in exhaustion.

The Temple to Amara loomed in the distance. It had taken

decades to complete. It seemed so far away. Hyron's old bones ached. Yet he had come this far. How could he back down now?

He walked across the way, beside the law courts and the archon's house. He passed between the towering pillars and beheld the inner chamber of the temple in all its glory.

The twilight was shining on the statue of Amara, forty feet tall. Her robe of gold had been melted down to pay for the Southron War, but even bare and un-ornamented, with snow-white marble, her majesty took Hyron's breath away.

An altar stood before the towering statue. The morning dove had begun to chirp; it knew its end was near. Hyron opened the cage and grabbed the white-feathered bird. "Please," said Hyron, "dearest Amara, mother of our city, let wicked Kunar lose…"

A priestess emerged from the shadows of the temple. She wore a crown of gold, forged into sunrays. Her chiton was white, with a blue sash. Her eyes were black, yet bright, and red lipstick stood out starkly against her pallid face. "A sacrifice for the goddess," she said.

"Yes." Hyron peered into the sweet morning dove's eyes. They were black as jet, tiny. The bird fit easily into his hand. Once, it had a mother. A father. *Yet the gods demand blood.*

"The goddess is displeased with her city," said the priestess. "Each year, the tithes dwindle. Farmers do not bring the fattened calf, but the skinny, mangy yearling… and you. I have not seen you here before, though you are second only to the archon."

"And yet I am here," Hyron said. "To invoke the goddess's blessing."

The priestess drew from her side a dagger, forged of steel. Its hilt was of gold, shaped into the goddess's face. A jewel was fixed to its crossbar, red as a beating heart.

The morning dove was looking back and forth, alarmed,

and struggling more violently than ever to rip itself free.

"'Sacrifices I do not desire. Blood, it does not please me.'" She was quoting from her holy book. "'Heroism is what I require. A brave face, a heart of steel. A hero, bright-eyed, sandaled, bare of hand… who can wrestle lions and win, who can change destiny's course and triumph, who can battle dark empires and draw the people to his name. Give me not the calf… give me not the dove. Give me a hero who fears not death. Give me a mighty champion.'"

She crossed the distance between them quickly. She pried open his hands and took hold of the white dove. "Your intent is enough. The goddess will give you what you seek. Go… all you have asked her, you will receive." She let the dove free and it flew away, darting past Hyron.

~

In the morning, as he sat eating breakfast in his home on Straight Street, his friend, the demiarch Agathion, burst in. His face was white and drained of blood.

"Kunar has won the election!" he shouted. "Kunar has won! *Kunar has won…*"

HUDOR'S PRISON, ALESIS, KORTHOS

Theron was awakened in his prison cell. The prison warden stood there with the keys to his shackles. "It is your death day," he said.

Theron had tried to put on a brave face. Yet there was no one alive who could face death without a small bit of fear. Surely even the gods in heaven were afraid sometimes.

More profound than the sinking feeling in his gut and the cold numbness in his hands and feet was the feeling of betrayal. The fact that his city had refused to pay his ransom reminded him that there was nothing to live for. There was nothing left. No one cared about him. No one wanted him. Eloesus had thrown him to the wolves, after he had saved the nation.

"Wait," said Theron.

The prison warden glared.

"I will die today," he said. "But first I will give you the code you seek. I want Thénai to burn."

The prison warden sighed. He was disappointed, apparently, that the execution would take a little longer; but knew his master Gaia would be delighted.

And moments later, she arrived in her gown of light gold cloth. "Give us the code," she said, "and you will be set free." She handed him a clay tablet and a stylus.

"I don't want to be free," Theron said. "I just want Thénai to burn."

With the stylus, he etched the code to the Hymnos Device:

J↑↑↓↓

"Can we, in good conscience, execute you," said Gaia, "when you have given us so much?"

"Forget your conscience," said Theron. "I will see you in hell."

At his words, Gaia smirked. "You are a strange one, Theron. But I will do as you ask…"

~

A crowd had gathered in Black Square to see Theron die. The executioner stood there near a chopping block, holding a massive cleaver in two hands. The executioner's face was hidden in a mask of black wool; his chest was bare and hairy, white as the moon.

Here in Black Square, all the most notorious criminals were slain—beheaded by an expert stroke to the delight of all who looked on. The seats were filled, some with two people, and others had packed the aisles. Hundreds more stood on rooftops overlooking Black Square, all to view the death of Theron, hero of the Southron War.

An artist had set his easel before the execution sight—all so that those who could not afford seats would be able to glimpse this injustice.

Once a Korthian had bragged to Theron, "Executions are the sign of a lesser civilization…" But Korthians were happy to execute people from different cities, or break the rules altogether when it suited them.

Theron, naked save a loin cloth of rawhide—his feet and legs bound—was kicked onto the hard stone pavement. He cried out as his knees flared with fiery pain. *Why*, he asked himself. He could have avoided this. He could have fled, even returned to Thénai—that ungrateful city which he had come to hate.

The executioner walked over with thunderous steps. "Any last words, vermin?"

"I hate Eloesus!" he shouted as loud as he could. "I wish the southrons had destroyed you!"

Loud jeers erupted from the crowd. They had come to detest this "amazon lover." Wild theories had spread throughout the country that he intended to hand over power to the amazons… to set up his wife Daphnë as "Queen of Eloesus."

The executioner grabbed Theron by his collared neck and lifted him up into the air. With loud, trudging steps, the executioner set Theron's head on the chopping block and pitched back his sword.

Chaos erupted in the crowd; loud screams were heard. A head struck the floor in front of Theron—the executioner's.

Theron looked up in a frenzy; an amazon stood there in chainmail and leathers. Two sabers were in her hands, dripping blood; their metal gleamed like twin fires in the sunlight.

A trail of bodies lay behind her. She kicked Theron to his feet and kicked a spear into his hands. "Come on!" she shouted. "We don't have time. Follow me!"

And so Theron followed as the crowd began to panic. Hoplites chased after Theron and his amazon savior as the crowd stampeded through the seats, trampling over each other.

He had been saved; but at what cost?

He was glad to be alive.

LIBERATION

The three hundred liberated women had reached the hills outside of Thénai. Each day the number of liberated women was growing; just a month ago only a hundred had joined Pygmalia on her midnight sojourns.

She had drunk a bottle of wine under the nose of her husband before departing. It had grown harder and harder to achieve drunkenness; but to achieve true Breckonasia—when you cared about nothing and no one—drunkenness was the first step.

And so, she and her sisters—the liberated women of Thénai—had brought with them a cartload of wine. Two oxen drew it as the liberated women sang and danced. At these hills, true liberty would be reached; all sorrow would be banished, all concern and worry destroyed. There would only be this, only now.

Pygmalia's husband had begun to grow concerned at her frequent disappearances; and yet the foolish husbands of Thénai did not realize how many of their women had achieved liberty.

"Liberty! Liberty!" Pygmalia shouted.

The cart had stopped and her sisters were grabbing bottle after bottle of wine. "Liberty! Liberty!" one shouted.

And yet Pygmalia was not as far advanced as she could; she had not achieved true Breckonasia. Her friend Demokrita had come very close.

A satyr had once approached Pygmalia in the cool of a summer's night, his eyes inflamed with lust, his cheeks red with passion. Yet she had resisted, even fought him off. The hairy goat-like legs, the curly flea-infested beard, had driven her far away from him.

She had not achieved Breckonasia. She had not slept with a satyr like Demokrita. But perhaps tonight—after many bottles of wine and chants to Lord Brecko of the Themurian grove—she would.

'THE WINTER WIND,' SOMEWHERE IN THE MIDDLE SEA

Theron loved Khloë with her kind gaze, with her long brown hair and her dark eyes. She had taken him on this ship with ample provisions; day after day she baked him bread in the ship's galley. Where the ship was going, not even Khloë knew, but it had left the harbor of Korthos and departed Eloesus altogether, sailing west.

And morning by morning, Theron's old strength was returning. The soft, warm bread, the small sips of Khloë's firewater, the scraps of salted meat, and the hours of sleep on a plush cot— all these were restoring his body in ways he could only imagine. In Hudor's Prison, the threat of life seemed greater than the threat of death. Now, Theron relished every moment.

The bread Khloë baked was soft and warm. The firewater at first had burned his tongue and caused him to pucker; but now he liked it better than wine. Better than any of this was Khloë's presence. There was life in her laugh, in her smile; and it was clear she was glad to be with him.

On the deck of *The Winter Wind,* Theron clung to the rails and let the water splash against him. The sky was bright blue and the sea a vibrant shade of azure. The winds were blowing strong as the ship continued its western path, spearing through the waves. The rowers above-deck and below could rest their arms; it seemed the holy gods had blessed their endeavors. No storm had overtaken them; only a strong wind, propelling them ahead.

Birds were circling overhead; a sign of shore.

Late in the day, excited shouts rang out—"Landfall! Landfall!" the sailors cried.

And Theron saw—beyond the waves—a marshland overrun with reeds, flat as a pan, and amid the swarming midges and mosquitoes, huts. He had gone further west than he had ever been.

After a journey of fifteen days, he had reached the land of Khazidea—a territory hostile to Eloesians, heavy under the southrons' sway.

~

It was another three days, sailing along the marshy shore, before true civilization appeared. Amid the reeds and black silt, crocodiles had shown their scaly faces and creatures like giant water cows—called hippopotamuses—fought and struggled against each other in the water.

The capital of Khazidea hugged the shore, in the midst of a shallow bay. A palace of red sandstone overlooked the city on a hill; a few buildings, also of sandstone, glowed like fire in the sun. But for the most part, the city was one of squalor, with mudbrick shanties and bare dirt roads.

Theron had escaped the country he despised; but was living in a place like this worth it?

~

Khloë guided him as he stepped off *The Winter Wind* and onto the docks. The sailors had begun to unload amphorae from below deck.

Nauseous, dizzy, and still slightly weak, Theron struggled along the shaky wooden platform. He had overestimated his strength. His stint in Hudor's Prison had done him damage he might never recover from.

~

The square in this city—surrounded by mudbrick shanties and overlooked by the red palace—was crammed with stalls and swarms of common folk.

The people were much shorter than Eloesians, and slender; their complexions were tan, almost red. Their language was completely foreign, and Theron had never felt like more of an outsider.

They seemed to ignore him as they went about their business, purchasing fresh fish and olive oil and Fharese carpets. But Theron would never consider himself an Eloesian again.

"What now, Theron?" Khloë put a hand on his shoulder.

"Revenge," Theron answered. "Sweet revenge."

A MILE OUTSIDE KORTHOS

Ever since the inventor drew up his plans, Gaia had waited eagerly for this moment.

She remembered just years ago—in the uncertainty leading up to the Southron War—when she had just been Politarch of Foreign Relations. The theft of the Hymnos Device, under the nose of the Thenoan government, had delighted everyone in Korthos. Experts on Old Dominion artifacts had testified of its great value; yet the code could not be thwarted, and the self-destruction mechanism could not be removed without the total obliteration of the device.

Now, all the government's work lay before her. Everything had come to fruition: all those funds set aside for research, the vials of quicksilver, the bars of electrum and lead, the precisely-forged steel pipes, costing a fortune. They would have a fully functioning war engine of the Old Dominion—a masterful weapon which could level Thénai and destroy the Thenoan League; and which could then destroy Kersepoli and bring Korthian rule throughout Eloesus. Tharta would kneel before Korthos, and Gaia's beloved city would be exalted forever.

Rogon stood beside her, lobster-like in his antennaed helmet and black plated armor. He had proven himself an excellent asset in the war; and he was thoroughly under Gaia's thumb. She had gained control of him; she owned him.

The Hymnos Device took up twelve feet in all—a mass of gears, pipes and wheels which towered above even Rogon. At the front of the device was a large ribbed head like a drill; and even before they pulled the lever, it whirred with energy.

A large slab of stone had been set before it for testing. If this Hymnos Device was like any other known to mankind, it would blast a hole through the stone, wide enough for an oxcart to pass through.

The archon Phaistion stood in the back of the machine; he had insisted on pulling the lever.

Luon, Chief Demiarch, began to set the code in motion. One by one he slid the proper symbols to their slots:

⌐↑↑⊣⊣

Gaia could see Phaistion was nervous. Something of such incredible power always had its risks. Gaia herself had made sure to step away a good distance, together with her Rogon. When treated without proper care, Old Dominion artifacts could prove deadly. Every once in a while reports would reach the city of a shepherd discovering some mechanism in a cave or underground and handling it carelessly—countless explosions and forest fires had begun that way.

Against her better nature, she put her hand in Rogon's; his gauntlet was cold to the touch.

Phaistion, pale and slick with sweat, counted down from ten. Even terrified, he would not back down and come across a coward. He knew just how important respect was to the position of an archon.

"Ten…" he said. "Nine…"

There were small bits of the engine that seemed different from others Gaia had seen.

"Eight… seven…"

The drill-like piece at the front was more pronounced and ragged. The body of the device was not cylindrical, but square in shape. Gaia fretted, biting her lips. She wondered if she had hired the best inventor, if all her work would end in a fiery explosion what would kill them all.

Her eyes turned to Rogon, then to Phaistion, then to all the demiarchs gathered. Her reputation was on the line, too; what would they think of her if she failed? She had lobbied them furiously, trying to convince them—as well as herself—that this engine was worth pursuing. If it failed, what would they think of her? Right now, she had them all about the throat; if she was proven a failure, she would be ignored as "that politarch's wife."

She held her breath as Phaistion prepared to pull the lever. She had no gods to pray to; she had not made a sacrifice in the temple since she was a girl. She had only her strength, her own intellect, to fall back on.

Phaistion pulled the lever.

The engine whirred to life. There was a loud shrieking sound which quickly became deafening; the crowd gathered rushed to put their hands over their ears. The drill at the front sparked with lightning; a beam began to form, bright and sizzling.

And then it died.

The drill lost its power. The sheaves of lightning turned to faint crackling sparks. The deafening noise vanished after a roar.

She had failed.

She cursed the engine, she cursed this earth.

She had brought all these demiarchs, all these politicians, out to see her work.

And she had failed.

Phaistion gawked at her. His disappointment was palpable.

"Something must be wrong with the design," said Gaia, and she glared at the one who had reconstructed the engine. The inventor, Pylades, had not failed her before. Now he would have hell to pay. Yes, the gates of hell would be opened to Pylades; he would rue the day he ever met Gaia. He would rue the day he ever took up his trade.

The demiarchs would no doubt talk about this amongst themselves. "That crazy Gaia," they would say. "That madwoman, she has led us astray."

In silent disappointment they began to filter out, making their way back to the city along the road.

Later, she found Pylades, cursing beside the engine.

"I did nothing wrong," Pylades was muttering. "Everything is right, I swear, by the holy gods."

Rogon, hulking over Gaia, grabbed hold of Pylades.

"You did do something wrong," Gaia said. "Something very wrong."

Pylades met Gaia's gaze; his eyes were wide with fear.

"You will be locked in the library," Gaia said, "with only bread and water to eat, until you find out what went wrong. We will have our war engine, one way or another."

"But Gaia," said Pylades, "I checked and double-checked everything… it can't be wrong… unless… unless…"

"You have heard your punishment," said Gaia. "I won't accept failure this time."

She would have her war engine. She had to; her entire career depended on it.

THE HOUSE OF ASSEMBLY, THÉNAI

The demiarchs' panic had not eased when the first meeting with Kunar was held.

Hyron had tried his best to keep everyone in order—but this outsider, this madman, had somehow won the trust of the Thenoan people.

Somehow, despite all odds and predictions, he stood before them now, fat and red-faced, making no friends and creating all manner of new enemies.

"The first order of business," said Hyron from his seat, "is the Breckonals."

Kunar eyed him, seeming unimpressed.

Hyron stood up; perhaps he'd be taken seriously now. "Women in the city are swearing allegiance to a cult. The number is only growing. They are meeting in the hills outside Thénai. Don't we remember a time not long ago when women were forbidden to drink wine? But now they are quaffing bottle after bottle, all for this new god… 'Brecko.'"

Kunar glared. His stare was so powerful, few could meet it head-on.

"We have greater things to worry about than women enjoying themselves," said Kunar. "What does it matter that they drink? Do you realize, my friend, that the Kersican League is growing… and we are lurching toward all-out war?"

Slowly, Hyron sat down. This archon had a more direct style than his predecessor.

Since the meeting began, he had achieved no greater insight into Kunar's mind. Still, his motives were an enigma. Still, he didn't know what to make of him. Why had he become archon? What did he have to gain?

"I believe some changes are in order in this House of Assembly," said Kunar. "Some of you, I believe, are extraneous. But that is a matter for another time.

"And I should have you know that a gift is being delivered to your House of Assembly this afternoon. My fellow Isteroi have decided to make a peace offering. Our peoples have fought against each other in the past; but this gift is intended to show we are of one blood."

The Isteroi were not considered Eloesians by many. Red-haired and red-bearded, they spoke a dialect of Eloesian but they were not the same. They were different. Their culture was inferior—or so the true Eloesians said. *They still have kings, and ideas of fealty and sovereignty. They are true barbarians. They are wild.*

"We need no gifts," said Hyron.

"But that is the beauty of a gift," answered Kunar. He smiled. "They are not needed."

Hyron eyed Kunar's friend and bodyguard, Tyrosion. He had taken a seat on a stool. Against protocol, he had in his possession two axes. Tyrosion would not let Kunar out of his sight. It was pathetic, really—fearing a group of two-hundred senile old men. If they had brought knives and hidden them under their cloak, could they truly cut a giant like Kunar down? They were frail and weak—Hyron, too. Their only ability was to never agree on anything. "The Assembly is useless," was a common refrain on the streets.

Kunar mostly sat out the day's constant bickering. The motion to ban the Breckonalian cult, like most other motions, came to a deadlock. Seventy-five voted against; one-hundred for, with twenty-five abstentions. The wives of Thénai would continue their misbehavior.

Hyron held a motion to discuss the army, but even that discussion broke along familiar lines. Half the demiarchs believed the army was just the right size; the other, led by Hyron, believed it was too small.

He was about to put forth a motion regarding something less controversial—the refurbishment of Amara's holy temple—when a horn blew.

"My Isteroi are here," Kunar said, "with their gift."

~

The statue was so tall it scraped the gate of Thénai as it rolled in on a platform.

Composed entirely of wooden planks, it was the likeness of a roaring bear. Its claws, its head, the spaces between its eyes—all were composed of planks, bent or nailed together, forming the smooth and polished likeness. Crowds gathered around it, gasping. Though ignorant, Hyron was sure they knew the bear to be the Isteroi national symbol.

Hyron also knew their talent for carpentry, but this—this, he could not believe. The statue cast a shadow as it rolled in— dragged by teams of oxen. Hyron followed the wooden bear as it made slow progress toward city square.

Wood would rot; but if anyone knew how to preserve a wooden statue, it was the Isteroi. Perhaps a layer of paint would do nicely; Hyron knew the artists of Thénai were already thinking of ways to improve it.

Where would this giant effigy rest—this ursine tower? Hyron would put forth a motion. Should they leave it by the quay? What about City Square? Or a smaller market square somewhere outside the city center? The motion would surely fail just like all others before them. Like everything else, it would prove a matter of great controversy.

On and on the tower of wood rolled, and it cast the shadow of a titan bear. What would the ancients think if they saw such a wonder? "Look!" they might say, "the great god Tyros has come to us in the form of a giant!"

The crowd of moderns seemed no less amazed. *How could they build such a giant statue,* they were surely thinking. *How could a carpenter make something so lifelike?*

The gargantuan statue teetered this way and that as it was rolled across the unevenly-paved road, but its foundation was sound. Not once did it buckle; not a single plank fell out of its place.

The crowd in the road swelled each moment as people took in the wonder from afar and ran to see the statue up close.

"What is that?" Hyron heard a child say.

"That is the god Tyros," his mother explained. "The Isteroi think he looks like a bear!"

The crowd was pressing in on Hyron. He should have hired hoplites to keep order. Each year, during Third Night, when the religious procession made its way up to Amara's holy temple, there would be fatalities. A crowd stepping over each other was surprisingly deadly.

Hyron thought he saw movement up in the hollow of the statue's eye as it wobbled back and forth in the wind. City Square was approaching. The Thenoans would thank the Isteroi for years to come; but they would still be called barbarians. *A barbarian carves fetishes from wood—a civilized person, from stone and metal.*

A crowd had already filled City Square, and the drivers of the oxen shouted and whipped people away. The wooden bear was higher than any building in the square; before its massive presence, Hyron and everyone gathered there were ants.

On and on the titan bear rolled. The crowd pushed in on

each other as the statue forged a path into them. At last, in the midst of the sweltering summer sun, the statue ground to a halt. There it stood, sunlight reflecting on its ears and gaping mouth. Each fang was carved of wood, whittled down to lifelike detail. Each paw was sanded and polished, each aspect of its face and muzzle.

And then a piece fell out the back of it; a trapdoor slammed down, and Isteroi warriors began pouring out. A horn blew. The crowd panicked and fled in every direction, trampling the weak underfoot.

The horn sounded again as the red-bearded Isteroi came running out of the "statue" with swords and axes. They had come to make their double agent, "Kunar," a king.

Hyron questioned what to do but found himself doing what was prudent—fleeing in panic. Only the goddess above knew what was to become of their city.

Thénai had been the victor of the Southron War, and now it had lost everything by betrayal.

OUTSIDE HAROON, KHAZIDEA

The red walls of the capital city lay behind Theron.

In summertime, back home, he had complained about the heat, but this was on an entirely new level. The heat here stuck to him like a blanket and he dared not move. Instead, dripping with sweat, he sat on a rock outside the city walls. There were no trees to shelter him, just Khloë standing there, tall and casting a shadow.

Over these days and weeks, Khloë had been his dearest companion, his greatest friend. She was different from Daphnë, though she had the same hard edges as all amazon women. This Khloë was more reticent than Daphnë, though she showed so much concern for his well-being. By the way she talked to him, Theron had learned of his heroic status in amazon circles—at least, among those amazons who had emigrated to the cities.

Yet he was not a "hero" anymore. The oracle's lie about him being Phillipidēs had been only a charade, a manipulation. He had put that old identity aside. He had given up the sword Pyrax and the Invulnerable Helm; now his two once-prized possessions were kept in the Thartan *herodium*. The hero shrine now held the hero's sword and helmet, even if it would never hold his bones.

"What now, friend?" said Khloë.

He had picked up on small bits of the language. Yet he could not shake his identity as a foreigner.

In Eloesus, no one thought twice about seeing a Fharese woman in a headscarf or a whiteskin barbarian trading goods in the market square. Here, Theron stood out among the short, slender, copper-skinned populace. For the most part, he was ignored. Yet the presence of foreigners was very minimal, and composed solely of traders.

"I think we will have to leave," answered Theron. He wondered what Khloë thought of that, after she had tried so hard to get him here. Theron had grand plans of joining the southrons and amassing a giant army, but now the thought seemed stupid, bordering on childish. Had he truly thought so highly of himself and of his abilities? Did he really think he could become a southron warlord?

Khloë nudged him with her foot. "Get up then. I suppose we have a ship to catch."

The Ten Cities accepted criminals and exiles. Perhaps they could make their way to Megaris and appeal for asylum. But that, too, seemed foolish. Ten Cities folk were considered the scum of the earth by other Eloesians.

Theron stood up and met Khloë's dark gaze. He knew they were running very low on money. She could ill afford another trip. If Theron was a betting man, he'd guess that he and Khloë became bandits and thieves before winter arrived.

~

They made their way through Haroon's rabbit warren of mudbrick homes and shops. Eventually they made their way out of the tunnel-like streets and into the open market square.

A procession was under way. A Khazidee was leading along a white bull, hoisting it by its collar. The altar, nothing more than a pile of stones, lay in view of a bright red temple.

The bull was stopped when it reached the edge of the altar. A priest emerged from the crowd, wearing a long purple robe and carrying a scepter. He began yapping in his native language and then, to Theron's surprise, he spoke in severely-accented Eloesian: "And to the eastron gods we also pray... to Tyros, to *Arphon* and *Amar*... save us from the Carceran Lion. Save us! Save us!"

The bull groaned as its throat was slit with a knife.

~

A ship was heading to the Blessed Isles, they discovered at port. A pair of merchants were bringing cargoes of southron spices, frankincense, myrrh and linens to that far-off land. It was as good a place as any to start anew. It was as good a place as any to build a new life.

The ship was leaving the following day. Khloë purchased a room at the inn.

Quietly, they sat and ate a meal of bread and water.

The table was low to the ground. Quilted tapestries on the walls did their best to hide the moldy plaster, but could not hide it completely. The floor was bare dirt where the wood had rotted away. Fragrant plants did their best to hide the smell of years of neglect and disrepair, but could not overpower everything.

Theron had never seen such squalor. He wondered if Khloë regretted saving him from the executioner's sword. She had been forced onto this adventure with him, an adventure which in all likelihood would end in destruction. Yet she said not a word. She guarded her feelings like a cat guarded its belly. To express oneself was a sign of weakness among the amazons; to show one's sadness, one's fears was the mark of a coward.

"Why did you leave Amazonia?" Theron asked.

Khloë met his gaze suspiciously. "I fought in the Battle of Korthos," she said. "I thought I had earned my citizenship."

"And you did," Theron said, "but why did you leave?"

"There are few opportunities for a young girl of my caste."

Theron wondered if she spoke the truth. But it was clear she did not want to say any more. He drank the rest of his water, ate the last bits of his bread, and retired to bed well before sundown.

In the middle of the night, there was a knock on Theron's door. He startled awake.

Khloë, sleeping on the bed close-by, leapt up and grabbed her saber from the floor.

Yet an assassin wouldn't knock. There was nothing to fear.

Theron approached and opened the door. Standing there was a Khazidee in a purple robe. Theron recognized him instantly: the priest who had been praying in the city square. He did not have his golden headdress or his purple raiment. His copper skin reflected a burnt ochre in the light of the candles.

He first spoke Khazidean, in that jabbering tongue, but quickly realized Theron didn't speak the language.

"I am from Eloesus," Theron answered him. He felt the shadow of Khloë approach. She had drawn her sabers.

In stilted Eloesian, the Khazidee attempted once more to communicate: "I sacrificed a bull before the gods… and I saw your face. You are the one chosen… the one chosen…"

Theron was ready to shut the door, but Khloë stopped him with her hand. "Chosen, for what?" she said.

"Come with me," said the priest.

~

The city—which after all this time, Theron learned was called Haroon—was circled by a large red wall. The priest—whose name, Theron, learned was Achiba—took him up the set of wooden stairs which lined the wall and up onto the battlements where they could survey the countryside.

It was night, but small villages built along the snake-like rivers were visible by their lights. Countless fields of wheat stretched all around; in the distance, Theron could see temples of red sandstone and fenced-in fields where cows were kept. The city of Haroon was a place of filth and squalor; but the lands around it were bursting with fertile ground. Hunger, they would never have to fear.

"Three years ago," said Achiba, "cattle began to die. Some farmers said a great beast was about; but the king and queen did nothing! They let the cattle and the sheep in their sheepfolds die off! Then people began to die, dragged off by the beast! Still the king and queen did nothing… and then their son the prince went hunting one day, and *he* was killed by the beast… the Carceran Lion. Only then did they decide to do anything… 'Kill the Carceran Lion,' they said, 'and I will give you anything, up to half the kingdom.' But none could kill the Carceran Lion… not even the best warriors in the land."

"And you think I can," said Theron.

"The gods said you could," answered Achiba.

But Theron had a dim view of sacrifices, and even less of supposedly "divine revelation." This dream or vision or whatever Achiba wanted to call it was the product of a deluded mind. If no one in Khazidea could kill this monster, who would reasonably think that Theron could? Theron had no supernatural powers, no divine blood; only common sense and a strong arm.

"The sharpest swords in the world can't cut the lion's flesh," said Achiba. "We have come to believe it is not of this world; it has come from the lowest depths of hell, from *Carceros*."

A lion from the underworld seemed exceedingly unlikely. So did everything else this Achiba was saying. And Theron had a ship to catch in the morning. He would be gone—whether Achiba liked it or not.

"Theron will fight your Carceran Lion," Khloë said.

Excuse me, Theron wanted to say.

"But if he kills the Carceran Lion, he will have more than half your kingdom," she answered. "He will have all your soldiers, all your armies—every sword-bearing man in Khazidea. He will have a fighting force to shake the earth."

EAST WING, HOUSE OF ASSEMBLY, KORTHOS

Despite the boldness of the city's actions, and the strength of the Kersican League, the city's position was more precarious than many believed. This, Gaia knew; and she had lost leverage even within Korthos' weak government. The embarrassment of the failed war engine lingered on, days later. The city's demiarchs and politarchs did not request her advice; in the halls of the Assembly House, they spoke in hushed tones and whispered amongst each other when she walked by. She had lost all credibility; and they had begun to push Rogon aside, as well.

A great coup in Thénai had produced elation in the Kersican League. The Isteroi barbarians had—with the aid of the elected archon—seized outright power over the city and imposed martial law.

And then, just as soon as the cries of celebration rang out, there was great concern. "This Kunar," a demiarch said to the Assembly, "is brash and strong. He is a fierce foe to the Kersican League… maybe fiercer than what came before. He is willing to risk blood."

And then, Gaia had begun to fear her own government falling apart. The ransom money for Theron—which they had stolen outright—was the source of a great conflict within the Korthian Assembly. None could agree how to spend it; at last, they decided that each archon would have a share for his personal profit. Forty *talents,* split two hundred ways, would enrich them beyond their greatest hopes… and squander a great opportunity for the city.

Rogon sat next to her in the privacy of the Assembly House's east wing, quiet as ever. Yet despite his silence, Gaia had come to know him—that he was very thoughtful and very observant. Despite her own fall from grace, Rogon still had influence in the Korthian government. His skill at war, his knowledge of the enemy, his keen insight on Thénai's weaknesses, and his connections to the Southern World—all of those were assets that could not be replaced.

Gaia, on the other hand, wife of a politarch, had seen her own influence dwindle every day. It was through Rogon and Rogon alone that she had any power at all. He was her only hope, her only saving grace. Without Rogon, she would have no influence on the Assembly or the Korthian government. Without Rogon, she would have nothing.

Rogon grasped her hand in his. He was, as always, too stoic to express concern.

Gaia had truly fallen from grace. And yet she had already determined what needed to be done. Rogon had been appointed a member of the Council of War. The plotting had already begun for battle. One by one they would pick off the weaker members of the Thenoan League.

Rogon was to lead an invasion of the isle of Nissos—and Gaia would go with him. Her husband did not know of she and Rogon's relationship; he would be enraged, but it did not matter.

To regain her power, Gaia's only hope was Rogon. "I am going with you," she announced. "The slavers of Nissos will be vanquished by both our hands."

Rogon refused to remove his armor, even in the most impractical of situations. Like a lobster he sat there in black plates of steel and dark antennae. "I advise against it. You have not seen war. You will not like it."

"I will learn to like it." Once, Gaia had seen a dog run over by a horse-cart, and the injury had been so traumatic to her, she dreamed about it for days. Yet queasiness and discomfort was nothing compared to regaining her influence, to restoring her fall from grace.

She had locked that lousy inventor in the library, and sent guards to watch over him. "You'll never leave," she had told him, "until you right your wrong." Gaia was under no illusions he would ever build a successful prototype. But his life from now on would consist of constant punishment.

"Come with me," said Rogon.

Gaia bristled at the command; usually it was she who ordered Rogon around. But as Rogon stood up, she decided to obey, wondering what he had in store.

~

Silently, Rogon led her through the swarming crowds of Heaven's Square, in view of the temples of Nix, Alabastros, Isdar and Tyros. The narrow side-streets led them further away from the heart of the city, until they reached the dirt ramps which led up to the High City. There he turned again down the dark maze of streets, where mudbrick houses were stained from years of smoke and dust. At last they arrived where Rogon was leading them—to a small square of dark basalt. Crowds had gathered here, lining the stands—Black Square, a place which Gaia had avoided since her youth.

Gaia, the daughter of a politarch and a scholar, had been taught the enlightened ways of the Korthian elite; it was universally agreed that public executions were barbaric and inhumane. Next to slavery, it had been considered society's greatest evil. "Why," she whispered.

"You say you can handle war," Rogon answered her. "I just want to make sure."

Gaia frowned. She knew in her heart that Rogon meant well; but she could not bear to look. "No."

"Then you won't be going to Nissos."

In the square, Gaia watched in horror as the black-hooded executioner approached the chopping block. In his pallid hands he held a cleaver which was already wet with blood. The ground around Black Square was similarly damp; the redness of the blood could not be seen, but it had gathered in pools of the porous rock. Gaia could not believe the savagery of the crowd, spending their idle hours watching the death of their fellow man.

A young man had been bound and gagged, with his head on the chopping block. "Hedon of Cobblers Street." A man stood in the shadows, some minor official of the city magistrate. "You have been sentenced to die for the murder of Theolaia, daughter of Timor of Fish Street."

The poor young man was shaking. Gaia wanted to break him free of his binds. But she could do nothing except watch. Quivering he sat there, whimpering through his cloth. A rich man might be able to pay his way out of execution; this Hedon was no doubt poor, and thus less equal in the sight of the law.

"Do you have any last words?" asked the official.

"I didn't mean to... I didn't see her... it was the horses who ran her over..."

The executioner swung his cleaver hard. Gaia cried out as the blade popped through bone and flesh and the head rolled off in a trail of blood. The crowd in the first row were sprayed with blood. Gaia fell back, lightheaded, and wilted like a flower.

She came to. Rogon was holding her up.

"Now do you see?" he asked her. "You can't handle war."

"I cannot handle the sight of bloodshed," answered Gaia, "but I will."

CITY PRISON, THÉNAI

In Thénai's darkest place, the sound of the waves crashing on the shore comforted Hyron. He had subsisted on bread and water for days. One by one, the demiarchs would go to their tribunal; one by one, they would die.

Hyron, now clothed in rags, sitting on a flea-bitten cot, cursed the gods for his situation. The priestess of Amara had promised him victory; within hours her pronouncement had proven a lie. *There are no gods*, Hyron thought. *There are no gods to curse.*

He cursed the barbarians, too—the Isteroi, who had proven beyond all doubt they were not true Eloesians. Red-haired, blue-eyed savages, they were; smelly and unkempt, uncultured and unlearned.

There was a rustling in the locks. The door opened, letting dim light flood in. An Isteroi stood there, a sword clipped to his side. Hyron spat at him.

Growling, the Isteroi stormed over and yanked Hyron by the arm, onto his feet. He bound Hyron's hands in rope and cinched it so tight, it cut his skin. "Come," yelled the Isteroi, and pushed him ahead, through the door, through the halls.

~

For the first time in days, Hyron entered the light of the sun; and he squinted at the bright blue sky and the now-vivid colors of everything which surrounded him. Ships were in the docks; ships of all kinds. In the far corner was a Fharese dhow, together with triremes of Eloesian make. Sailors were hauling amphorae and crates into town by the cart-load. The Isteroi invaders had lobbed off the head of government and replaced it with their own; nothing else seemed to have changed.

A band of Isteroi roughed up Hyron and pushed him ahead. *This is the end,* he thought. Yet he felt no fear; he was only numb.

~

The road from the port through the Long Walls was packed with people. Indeed, it seemed like nothing had changed.

The road opened up, eventually into City Square. The reconstruction had been finished: the dull white stone replaced with vivid mosaic patterns of red, green, blue and white. Yet where the statue of a hoplite had been planned to honor the fallen in the Southron War, an abomination stood.

There, gleaming in white marble, was the effigy of Kunar, hand outraised, clutching the helm of a war-chief. *His arrogance knows no bounds.* There was no limit to his delusion.

The Isteroi captors let him gawk at the marble visage. Then one laughed and pushed him on.

~

Overheated and dripping with sweat, Hyron reached the top of the High City. The law courts he had known were flanked with statues of Kunar. The temple of holy Amara, where he had prayed and offered sacrifices, was being rebuilt and rededicated to Tyros, god of war.

Yet the Isteroi pushed him onward, heedless of his feelings, heedless of his exhaustion. Like slave-drivers, they forced him ahead until—panting—he collapsed on the marble floor of the court of law.

Kunar stood there, gloating, arrogant. His face was as red as ever, but he had a smirk on his face which Hyron had never seen before.

On Kunar's head was something despised by Eloesian democrats: a crown of gold. Kunar had been elected archon; he had declared himself king. "Hyron, friend," he said.

Hyron scowled.

"I have suspended the Assembly. The Assembly House, I am turning into an armory. All your *Strategoi* have been executed—your soldiers answer to better masters, now. And I have you where I want you. Bowing before your king."

Hyron stood up on his weak, old legs. He spat in Kunar's direction.

Kunar laughed. "I offer you a chance to live, Hyron. All other demiarchs are dead, save you. If you will acknowledge me as king, supreme ruler of Thénai, without equal, without compare, I will let you live."

"Never," answered Hyron. "I will drink of hemlock before that happens."

"Will you," said Kunar. He motioned with his fingers.

His thugs backed away.

"I offered the same to all your fellows," answered Kunar. "One by one they agreed… and I killed them. Every other demiarch is rotting in the cemetery. But you… you alone showed character."

Kunar had killed all of Hyron's friends. He despised this Kunar, more than anyone else in the world.

"Get him clothes," said Kunar. "Release his binds. Cut his hair and give him some food. We have found our newest court advisor."

But nothing Kunar said could take away what he had done. Hyron could never forgive him. Kunar would come to regret his choice.

KHAZAN RIVER DELTA, KHAZIDEA

Khloë watched as Theron crept through the bushes like a cat ready to pounce. The Khazidees had given him a sword which had supposedly been blessed by the high priest; but Khloë had learned not to trust in amulets and talismans. This sword—broad and thick in the manner of Khazidea, forged of steel—would fare no better than any other.

Khloë took his cue and bent down through the brush. They had more to fear than the Carceran Lion. Crocodiles were among the deadliest animals of all, though they shied away from humans; even more so the water cow which Khazidees called "hippopotamus." They were on the edge of the river; the ground was muddy and thick, the path uncertain. Yet the tiny villages, here—ten miles from Haroon—had reported seeing the Carceran Lion stalking its prey. It was bound to be here, somewhere; so Theron with his cleaver, and Khloë with her sabers, searched silently, crouching in the brush.

A crocodile splashed in the water and dove away as Theron approached; Khloë caught sight of only a ripple of scales. It was dusk but the heat was thick as a blanket, more oppressive than the hottest day Khloë had ever faced back home. She had left her armor behind, leaving her body exposed; but it was a small thing to risk compared to the Khazidean sun.

Across the river was a pasturage where cows nibbled at the grass, swatting flies with their tails. Rows of wheat, still green, covered the fertile soil everywhere, like it was grass. This was truly the breadbasket of the world, a place where the harvest was bountiful and the farmers never had to work for long.

Theron held up his hand. "Hush," he said.

Khloë looked around and spotted movement in the reeds. A dark shape had emerged, stalking through the earth.

Then it emerged—a person, swatting flies as he eyed the river cautiously. He had set out nets for fish.

Theron sighed. Khloë could sense his disappointment.

When the moon arose, and the stars were twinkling, no further sign of progress was made. For days they had searched for the Carceran Lion; now, having failed so often, Khloë had begun to nurse doubts that the beast existed at all. *Perhaps,* she thought, *this is all some practical joke. Perhaps the people of Haroon are laughing at us now. "Those silly eastrons! Those silly eastrons! Ha!"*

A scream lit up the night, piercing in its timbre. "Help!" someone cried in the Khazidean language. It was coming from the distance, across a river.

Immediately Theron dove in and swam. Khloë swallowed her fear of crocodiles and followed.

~

Along the sandy banks of a sinuous river, in the cool of the night, lay the remains of a village. Thatched houses of wattle-and-daub lay in disarray, their roofs caved-in, their walls missing, and blood drenched the grass. The bodies of dozens lay nearby—and far off and skulking, a dark shape made its presence clear in the outlying fields.

MELEK VILLAGE, KHAZIDEA

Theron had seen a lion once, when—on Third Night—the demiarchs of Thénai brought forth an exotic menagerie. Once, the lion—the greatest of the great cats—had prowled the countryside of Eloesus, but they had been hunted to extinction.

The creature he saw, towering above the rolling wheat, was nothing like the lion he had seen in the menagerie. This lion was taller than Theron. Its head was the size of a cart-wheel. Its mane was inky black like midnight. Its head and body were cadaver white.

The eyes of the Carceran Lion glinted green in the pale moonlight. It seemed to be smiling at Theron, almost mocking.

It batted its paws in the ground. It turned to face Theron, revealing its black-striped hind legs.

The night, which once had been silent, was filled with a low growl.

From behind, Khloë hurled three chakrams; they whistled by Theron's ear in quick succession. The tiny discs bounced off the hide of the Carceron Lion, shaving off hairs but failing to pierce the skin.

It became clear Theron had undertaken a fool's errand. But he tried to remind himself of the heroes of old. Phillipidēs and Helēmon and Megara—all were descended of gods—but they faced danger with a stern gaze and hearts of iron.

He had no chance to conjure his bravery. The Carceran Lion bounded toward him, moving like a machine. It dove at him; Theron dove under it. Theron slashed its hind leg with his sword but made no more than a scratch.

The lion turned around and roared; its roar resounded through the fields and echoed through the valleys. Its roar sent crocodiles splashing away and caused owls to take flight. Its roar shook the foundations of the earth.

The lion pounced again, and again Theron ducked away. He struck the lion with all his might, with every ounce of strength he had in him.

The blade broke in two on the impenetrable hide.

The Carceran Lion roared again. In a moment, it turned around and pounced. This time, its paws caught on Theron's flesh.

The hilt of the broken sword was still in Theron's hand.

Khloë screamed and began slashing wildly with her sabers.

As the Carceran Lion began to rake its steely claws across Theron's chest, Theron beat the creature's head wildly with the hilt of his blade.

As his flesh was torn open, Theron raised his sword in desperation and drove the iron pommel into the lion's head. There was a loud crack as the skull fractured. The lion yelped and backed away.

Then it turned its tail and ran.

Theron was dripping with blood. Blood had soaked his tunic and his breeches; and where there were massive lacerations to his chest, more poured out by the second. He had turned faint.

He laughed at the irony. He had discovered the lion's weakness. And now he would die.

But Khloë had approached, and stooped over him. Out of her pack she produced cloths and bandages. She mopped up the blood and firmly pressed the bandages to Theron's massive wounds.

"I am going to die," said Theron.

"Not if I can help it," she answered.

She grabbed from her pack a knife and a needle. From her

belt she unhooked a canteen.

"Drink," she demanded.

And Theron obeyed. The firewater burned him as it coursed down his throat. He felt its effects quickly; he grew numb, placid, happy.

And then Khloë poured the firewater on his wounds. Theron screamed.

With the needle and thread, and her knife, she began to sew his wounds shut. Theron cried from the pain; the firewater wasn't enough to numb him. He cursed as Khloë did her work. The pain reached its apogee, and everything went black.

~

It was morning and the sun was already burning down on Khazidea.

Still weak, still tender with pain, Theron set his eyes on Khloë. She had become beautiful to him. All that helpfulness, all that loving care and she had become the most beautiful woman in the world.

She grabbed his hand and gingerly helped him up. The pain coursed through Theron like fire, but he ignored it.

~

Later in the day, they came to a village. "Build me," Theron told the carpenter, "a club of tamarisk wood. Weight it with lead."

And all day the carpenter fashioned this weapon from the finest of wood. When he had carved it in full and watched the molten lead cool, he handed it to Theron in exchange for all the money in Khloë's coinpurse.

Theron turned to Khloë and smiled. "We have a lion to

kill."

OUTSIDE NISSOS

Weeks later…

Gaia's nerves were overwrought as she viewed the city of Nissos. Her stomach was fluttering. She had demanded to be here, against the protests of the Assembly. And she had achieved her goal.

Skirmishes with the Thenoan Navy had been largely avoided. Under the nose of warships, ten thousand hoplites had been ferried to shore. Ten thousand was all they needed—or so Gaia had been told.

The walls of the City of Nissos lay before her; they had stood for hundreds of years. Here, people were put on display and sold as tools. Slaves from the far north and the far south, from the east and the west, had been gathered here and shipped to ports of call. Slaves of all skills and all complexions could be found, from scribes to farmhands, from swarthy southrons to whiteskin barbarians. All those human lives, all those souls, displayed on a platform, given a price.

The army had gathered around Nissos' golden walls. The Nissoi had posted archers and hoplites on the battlements but as the ten-thousand Korthians began to gather, Gaia could sense a change in the air. The archers on the wall looked nervous. They knew they had no chance.

And from the trees of the island, Korthian soldiers had begun to do what they knew best; with saws and hammers and nails, they had begun to fashion instruments of siege: battering rams and catapults. The walls of Nissos would break; the gates would splinter and crack. There would be no escape. There would be no recovery.

The gates rolled open. A man rode out with a white flag of surrender.

The Korthian hoplites looked to Rogon.

Rogon looked at Gaia. "Who better to negotiate than our Ambassador?"

~

"Ambassador" had once been a paltry title. Gaia had exerted all forms of influence she possessed to turn it into something meaningful. Before the Hymnos Device embarrassment, she had been welcomed at Assembly meetings and even served as a politarch; yet there were things Gaia could not overcome. As a woman she could never hold the office of demiarch or archon; she would never be invited to dinner parties and symposiums, and many men of the older generation looked down on her for "straying so far from home." It was no matter; she would prove them all wrong.

Beyond the golden walls was the City of Nissos, a city of broad thoroughfares painted in white stone, towering homes of gleaming white and—in the distance—villas gleaming over the seaside. All this wealth, all this beauty, had been paid for on the backs of slaves, on the countless silver pieces, the souls purchased for a price.

Under siege, the market square was empty; but the traces of the dark trade were visible. There were cages set up on platforms and manacles anchored to the stone. There were stands for moneychangers, which allowed every currency under the sun to be used to purchase slaves—southron and eastron, islander and mainlander, would find what they looked for if they sought the souls of the lost and abandoned.

Gaia was not one for compassion and tenderness, but she could not help but bristle when she saw a slave. Was there any fate worse than slavery? It was worse than death.

On a rocky outcrop, the house of the Prince of Nissos

overlooked the sea. Its colonnades and gardens were visible from any point in the city; its white walls and pillars, its sparkling red roof, its towering bronze fence—all seemed to look down on the city below.

~

For ages, the princes of the House of Narcissi had ruled the city and its island. They did not recognize the democracies of Thénai and Korthos as legitimate governments. When the commonbloods rose up and slew their kings, the Royal Narcissi had cut off all contact. Even now they spoke only grudgingly to their counterparts.

Yet this prince met Gaia with a bow. He was young, slender, handsome, wearing a blue robe of fine wool. On his head of curly brown hair was a silver circlet. His fingers gleamed with jeweled rings; a ruby amulet was around his neck. He smelled of myrrh.

His throne was of gold, festooned with rubies and sapphires and diamonds. A mosaic floor covered the entire room, depicting the sea-god Lornos. The windows were trimmed with gold and silver. Against the bright-white walls were ancient masterworks of art—paintings hundreds of years old, no doubt originals, which would fetch hundreds of gold pieces—if they were for sale.

"What do you want of us, Ambassador?"

This young man—whom Gaia learned was named Prince Alexis—was not much more than a boy. He was impressionable. "The City of Nissos has pledged loyalty to the Thenoan League," stated Gaia.

"Yes." Alexis glanced away. "We pay Thénai every year from our treasury. They will not let us leave."

"The Kersican League will welcome you with open arms," Gaia said, "and whatever you pay Thénai, we will ask half that. We will guarantee your protection. We will ensure your city never falls into their hands."

Alexis sighed. In his mannerisms and his speaking he was immature; the princedom and all its demands were far too much for him. Gaia was barren, but she felt a motherly instinct with this young child. She wanted to help him, to shape him, to mold him. "I guess we have no choice," he said.

"And you will free all your slaves," said Gaia. She could not believe she said those words. Yet they had been building in her, breaking out from her shell of cynicism. *You are the most ruthless politician I have ever met,* Rogon once said—but she had become an idealist.

"I don't think we can do that," said Prince Alexis—timid, nervous.

But Gaia had made up her mind. "You will," she told him. "You have no choice."

THE HOUSE OF THE ARCHON, THÉNAI

All this time spent with the Isteroi, and Hyron thought no better of them. In fact, he had only grown to hate them more. They had trashed the house of the archon; they used the busts of Ansolon and Megara as target practice. They shot their bows at paintings. They spent all their time guzzling wine.

Kunar had begun to grow out his beard like the rest of his Isteroi thugs. He claimed "he could not make good decisions without a few bottles of wine."

Thus Hyron stood among them, sober, amidst their squalor. The tattered remains of paintings hung lopsided on their walls. Bits of broken marble were all that remained after arrows pierced the statues of Gnosor and Hordo.

For their days-long drinking parties, they had brought a special game from their barbaric homeland. With their thumbs, they would hook the handles of clay pots, and then toss them at targets to watch them shatter.

Kunar bothered Hyron little. Hyron was to keep the city running, to ensure the military was expanded and well-paid-for. Kunar—in his rare periods of sobriety—had spoken of his plans to drag the Kersican League into outright war.

"We have an alliance with the mighty Isteroi now," he had told Hyron. "Now, they don't stand a chance."

He had believed Kunar at that time, a week ago. Now—standing amid the wreckage of the House of the Archon, as Kunar and his Isteroi tossed clay pots at a target they had carved into the wall—there was little doubt. The Thenoan League would fail under the weight of Kunar's drunkenness, debauchery, and foolish decisions.

Seeing the spectacle, Hyron almost forgot why he had come up all this way.

Kunar was lying on a wine-stained couch with two courtesans by his side. He tossed a clay pot and missed the target by more than a foot. He cursed.

"Your Majesty," Hyron said. The words were always difficult to say, though Kunar had forced them out of him. "An informant has told us that Nissos is under siege…"

"Forget it," Kunar said. "Tell me tomorrow. I have pots to throw."

Hyron bit his lip. Ever since the Isteroi had invaded, he'd kept a dagger clipped to his belt. How easy it would be for Hyron to plunge the blade into Kunar's heart. At the very least, he could hold the sharp edge to Kunar's throat and force him—for once—to stop drinking.

Hyron cursed and stormed off. He prayed for Amara the avenger to strike Kunar dead.

~

Kunar was a drunkard; Kunar was a fool. That much was evident. The Isteroi were good warriors—strong and tall, and as fearless as lions—but they lacked leadership and wisdom.

Nissos had joined the Thenoan League as soon as the Southron War ended. Each month, it paid its dues to the treasury at Choros. The loss was severe, more severe than Kunar—in his pathetic state—could ever hope to realize.

As Hyron made his way down the steep road from the High City, the weight of the city's problems seemed to lie upon his shoulders. A storyteller had once spoke of the hero Helēmon who—after vanquishing a demon—sailed on a ship to the far end of the world, to Dys. *There, a giant stood, holding up the sky on his back.*

Helēmon, a hero born of a god, had held up the sky on his back for thirty days and thirty nights—but Hyron, well advanced in age, had no such strength. Somehow, he had to solve the city's problems. Somehow, he had to overcome the Kersican League and Kunar—that fat oaf who dared call himself "king."

He was halfway down the steep downward slope when a hand caught him off guard. He turned to strike the one who almost tripped him—and saw a face he recognized.

A woman stood there in a white chiton, with a blue sash. Her dark eyes, her red lips, and her coiffed hair identified her as the priestess of Amara. "They are defiling the temple," she said. "The goddess is displeased."

Though she was a priestess, a servant of the holy gods, Hyron glared at her. He could not forget her injustices and her lies. "I offered you a dove," he said. "You said the goddess would grant my wish—and yet Kunar won. Kunar has declared himself king!"

Perhaps Hyron's fury was undeserved. Perhaps this woman really believed her prophecy. She did not realize the gods she served were frauds—figments of imagination, fervent wishes for the unlucky in an unjust world.

"That is what the goddess told me." The woman looked less regal without her sunray crown. "She also told me 'there is one coming. There is one who will claim his birthright.' You must prepare the temple for him. Drive out the priests of Tyros… re-consecrate it on Third Night."

Third Night was almost a month away, in the waning days of summer. There was no chance he would ever listen to what this woman said, ever again. Her prophecies were lies; everything she had ever told him was untrue.

Kunar had driven out Amara's priestesses; he had melted down the gold raiment of the goddess's statue. For now, and for the future, Hyron would do nothing about it. It was a temple of

Tyros now. *Let the goddess solve her own problems.*

THE DESERT, OUTSIDE KHAZIDEA

Theron was no tracker. Khloë had only a little better experience.

But no skill was required. Along the barren, sandy ground of this desert, the trickle of blood left by the injured lion was as easy to read as a bold red line.

The lush wheat fields, watermelon patches and pasturages had vanished. The well-watered greenery was gone, replaced with a yellow, rock-strewn desert and a burning, merciless sun.

Their water supplies were almost empty. The peril of their situation was evident, and Khloë made a point of reminding him. But Theron had decided. He would not rest until the Carceran Lion was slain, and its cadaver-white skin was flayed from its body.

The sun was burning down on them. Theron's skin had turned red and flaking; Khloë was no better. His skin burned from the sun; his tongue was parched, but he had to conserve their water.

Theron had counted three days since leaving the green abundance of Khazidea. At night, he had dreamed of the quaint villages, rich with the aromas of baking bread. Food had not only been plentiful, but also freely offered. Without spending a single *thalos,* Khloë and Theron had eaten well. In Khazidean villages, they were put up every night in comfortable lodgings. Villagers would serve them great platters of seared lamb seasoned with cumin or dill; bowls of thick pottage and haunches of crispy pork. They would serve hot loaves of bread sweetened with honey alongside jar after jar of beer. They cooked with beer and they ate with beer. As an Eloesian, Theron had been taught to savor the sacred "fruit of the vine" and all the varieties of wine, but how good was it to see the cup of golden liquid, bubbling up to the surface, erasing all the fears and anxieties of travel.

In midday, the sun had grown so oppressive Khloë begged, "Look—a tamarisk…"

The tree which offered shade to so many a traveler stood out among the barren sand and rock. Alone it stood, green against yellow and gray. In the distance there were tufts of grass. *There is water nearby.* "No," said Theron. "Let's go on."

Khloë was too tough to admit she was thirsty, or hungry, or weak. She would never disagree.

And so they continued on. Another tamarisk appeared in the distance, and grass became the norm rather than a rarity.

Then the ground leveled off and dropped into a deep chasm.

~

In the valley below, there were piles of bones. Some, Theron could identify—a boar, a cat, a lion. Others were so large they defied belief.

And in the center of this bone-yard was a dark tunnel, twisting down into the earth.

"The entrance to Carcerus," Theron said. He had taken little stock in tales of the underworld, considering them stories to enliven a campfire. But he had begun to believe.

At the entrance, the Carceran Lion had collapsed. Its white chest was heaving with strained breath. It had attempted to escape into its home, but the wounds had caught up with it. Three days and many miles later, the wound which Theron dealt had finally done it in.

Up close, Theron could see what distinguished this beast from other lions. In girth, it was twice the size of an ox. Its paws were the size of cart-wheels. Its eyes were not feline, but reptilian—like the cold eyes of a crocodile on the Khazan. Those eyes strained against the sunlight. Clearly, daylight was anathema to it. Yet Theron—pursuing him like a good hunter—had forced it to continue. The Carceran Lion never had an opportunity to nurse its wounds.

It snarled and bit at him when Theron touched the inky-black hairs of its mane. Its teeth touched Theron's finger, but were too weak to sink in.

This beast, sent from the depths of the earth below, had failed in its mission to destroy the daylight-dwellers. Was he sent by Kronos? Gods only knew.

The blade of a sword would not kill it. Its bones were its only vulnerability.

With his club, Theron beat the Carceran Lion's head with skull-snapping force. He struck again, and it fell unconscious.

"How will we prove we killed it?" asked Khloë.

"Hand me your knife," Theron answered.

With enough sawing and deep cuts, Theron found a weak part of its hide. He removed the skin from its head, and cut away bits of the mouth.

Then, like a helmet, he donned the Carceran Lion's head.

Khloë staggered back. "You look like a hero, of old."

In the waters of a pool nearby, they filled their waterskins. With rocks, bones and earth, they sealed up the hole leading into Carcerus; then, with spirits high, they headed east to Khazidea, to receive their reward.

THE BLUE PALACE, NISSOS HARBOR

Bedlam in the City of Nissos.

What had Gaia expected? Prince Alexis had not taken the suggestion of "freeing the slaves" well.

And now she was a hostage. Against protocol and all laws of war, the Ambassador had been taken prisoner. And here she sat, near a window overlooking the city, her hands bound in cuffs, guarded by two hoplites.

The lull in fighting had ended last night—no doubt, when Rogon learned of her capture. Now the catapults were launching stones into the city proper, the gates were under assault, and ladders fell on the Nissian walls.

The City of Nissos had never fallen. Its towering gold-colored walls were virtually impossible to scale. Its army was small, but formidable.

She imagined what the Assembly in Korthos would say. *You are a madwoman, sitting here with your principles. You threw it all away, for the sake of the slaves.* But Gaia would not bend or break. Nissos would fall eventually. Every chain would be broken, every manacle torn off. Every human, treated like an object, would again have a voice.

~

Just a mile away—but in situation, countless leagues from his lover—Rogon was cursing at his men. Arrows flew from the top of the walls in constant succession. A battalion of hoplites had splintered the gate with a battering ram, but made little more progress. The Nissians were far outnumbered. They would fall soon enough, but the fact they had resisted irked him to no end.

And they had taken Gaia. The fact motivated Rogon little. He had taken stock of her manipulative ways. Power, the one thing she desired above all else, was a factor in everything she did—even her own love.

And yet Rogon had his own motivations. Gaia thought he was a brute, a man who was simple-minded yet a lion on the battlefield. But he was more cunning than she knew.

"Forward!" Rogon shouted. More hoplites took up the battering ram and renewed the assault on the gate. The wood buckled under the force of the ram, but did not yield. It was well-crafted, almost impenetrable. But Rogon had learned—over his many decades of war—that no gate was strong enough to resist forever.

~

Late that same day, as the gate showed signs of splintering and the morale of the enemy was faltering, a sight Rogon had desperately hoped not to see befell him: hundreds of ships bearing the blue-and-gold laurel wreath flag of Eloesus. The city's defenders would be reinforced. Nissos would not fall. It was hopeless, now.

But maybe not. Rogon did have one last move to make.

THE BLUE PALACE, NISSOS HARBOR

When she saw the hundreds of hoplites leaving the Nissian port, sent from Thénai, Gaia could have panicked. She could have buckled under pressure; surrendered all. Instead, she was more determined than ever. She would prevail. *I always have. I always will.*

The Thenoan hoplites in their blue capes and bronze helms were making their way to the wall. There they would join the battle. Could Rogon wrest victory from this complete disaster? Gaia had her doubts. He was a mighty warrior, stronger than anyone in the Thenoan army, but he was more brawn than brains. He had consolidated power in Korthos; he had strengthened the Korthian army. But in a contest between brute strength and strategy, strategy always won out.

Without him, she would still prevail. Even if their force was defeated, she would make a way. She had always won. She had always managed to eke out a victory.

Hours after the ship arrived, there was a commotion beyond the door of her makeshift prison. "We have the ambassador here," said the voice of Prince Alexis.

And then the young prince entered, followed by a man in full armor.

His breastplate was forged into the shape of muscles. Over his arms he wore bronze greaves, and in his gauntleted hand, there was a sword. In the other he held a helmet with a blue horsehair crest.

His hair was dark, specked with gray. His eyes were intense, his nose aquiline. This was a man of great importance. The blue color of his helm indicated he came from Thénai.

"Ambassador," said Prince Alexis. "This is our savior."

"A pleasure," answered Gaia.

The man's stern look did not change with Gaia's smile. "Nicomedē of the West Island Command. There has been a truce between the Thenoan and Kersican Leagues. It is clear you want war."

This Nicomedē quite clearly held himself in high regard, judging by the way he carried himself. He was a Strategos, a commander of soldiers. Yet Gaia sensed he was not nearly so wise as he thought.

"You will have war," continued Nicomedē. "Nonetheless, you are an ambassador. You may return to your army if you wish… or we can take you to the mainland, to Thénai…"

The enemy city was preferable to certain slaughter. *Poor Rogon.* She would find a way to manipulate the situation to her advantage. She would find a way to take Nissos for herself, and all its wealth. She would break the binds of the slaves; they would call her "Gaia, the Mother of Liberty."

To Thénai she would go. There was no point in shedding a tear for Rogon. There was only time to plot her next move.

OUTSIDE THE CITY OF NISSOS

Rogon had developed a bond with these hoplites. In times such as these, when defeat seemed certain, their iron-clad trust of him and unit cohesion propelled them on.

The catapults had run out of stones to throw; as a battalion of hoplites scoured the countryside for more, they had begun to load the buckets with the bodies of fallen Nissians. They flung the pierced corpses into the city, where they would surely burst on impact and terrify the residents. No doubt the defenders on the wall had been rejuvenated and renewed with morale when the Thenoans arrived. Rogon would do whatever he could to chip away at it again.

So much of the outcome of a battle depended on a feeling of inevitability, of momentum. When panic overtook the ranks, defeat was assured.

Quietly, he had urged hoplites to gather bundles of sticks. He had ordered others to scour the villages of Nissos Island to see whether they possessed quicklime, mercury, and coal.

It was an ancient recipe which could turn the tides of battles. The method of its making had been a closely guarded secret. The sticky fire, which could never be extinguished until it consumed all in its path, was known to the magi in Rogon's homeland. The magi had refused to tell even the Fharese king how to make the "all-consuming fire," but Rogon had uncovered the recipe despite all the efforts at secrecy.

Magi knew how to create all kinds of fire: powdered fire, fire which could burn in water, fire which ignited on contact with water, fire which produced poisonous smoke, and more. All of their knowledge was hidden, kept completely secret on pain of death. But one recipe had evaded their careful suppression—the one they called quickfire, which required rare ingredients in exact amounts.

It was their only hope.

A horn blew. More ships appeared on the horizon. The battlements on the walls were crowded with hoplites. Rogon's forces—once quadruple the size of the Nissians—were now outnumbered.

"Athra," Rogon prayed silently, "give me your fire."

HAROON, KHAZIDEA

Khloë had expected a joyful reception from the Khazidean citizens of Haroon. Instead, seeing Theron wearing the lion skin, they were met with looks of disgust and horror. In this squalid metropolis in the hinterland of the world, the people of Khazidea had received help from afar—and now they scorned that very help, help which they did not deserve.

She had no doubts it was the sight of Theron wearing the lion-skin on his head. These city-dwellers had never seen the Carceran Lion up close; nor did they appreciate the sacrifices Theron had made. Safe within these city walls, their lives were never in danger. They never had anything to fear.

But still, shouldn't they greet Theron with celebration? Not these glares.

The Khazidees worshipped the goddess Isdar, queen of fertility and pleasure, above all others. In the center of town, overlooking the harbor, was a red temple of brick and sandstone. A spiked iron gate forbade entry.

There were two warriors standing behind the iron grills. They were shirtless and muscular, wearing chainmail skirts and bearing cleavers. Their heads were bald save a black ponytail. The Khazideans called this ancient order of warriors the Anakhil.

Yet even these hardened warriors withdrew slightly at the sight of Theron in a lionskin.

"What do you want?" one of them said in the Khazidean tongue which—over these weeks and months—Khloë had begun to learn.

"I demand to speak to Achiba," said Theron.

The priest had promised them the world if they slew the

Carceran Lion. Khloë turned her head; she saw a vast crowd of peasants and street people gathered around them. Perhaps none had dared speak so rudely to the priest's men before—none but "the warrior woman and the man in the lion's skin."

"Achiba will not speak to you," said the Anakhil.

"I killed the Carceran Lion," Theron said. "I demand my reward."

Several of the street people gasped; in the tense silence, Khloë could hear every minute sound, every foot shifting, every strained breath.

Khloë acted instantly; she knew Theron better than anyone. She knew what he wanted. She hurled two chakrams and the discs embedded deep into the Anakhil's exposed flesh. Theron grabbed the neck of one before he sank to the floor; he grabbed the set of keys, and opened the gate.

The street people did not fight them; beneath their fear was quiet delight. None had ever stood up to the priest's men before now… none before the amazon and the hero in the lion's skin.

~

They found Achiba in the temple yard. As Khloë and Theron burst in, prostitutes fled inside—women covering themselves with cloths or nothing at all. In Khazidea, it seemed, there were different ideas about religion. To be fertile was to honor the Fertile Goddess; to be chaste or celibate was considered sin.

To his honor, Achiba did not run or try to flee. As the color drained from his place, he merely stood there, frozen, unable to escape his fate.

"You said I could have an army," said Theron. "You said I could have anything, 'up to half the kingdom.'"

"You killed it." Achiba's eyes were wide and shallow with

panic. "I didn't think it was possible…"

And then, Khloë realized what had been happening all along: Achiba had formed some dark pact with the Carceran Lion. He had thought it invincible. He had sated its hunger with sacrifices; perhaps he thought Eloesians and amazons would taste the best of all.

"Where is my army?" Theron was shouting, now. "Where is it?"

"I promised you things I cannot deliver," said Achiba. "The king and queen will not acquiesce… I am sorry."

Theron crushed Achiba's skull with the club. The priest sank to the floor.

And he turned to face Khloë, his skin speckled with blood. He was frowning. *He is sad… sad about what he just did.*

And yet, though they had defiled the temple, Theron did not hesitate to rob it. A year's worth of tithes and offerings were found in a vault in the inner sanctum of the temple. They grabbed what gold they could stuff in their coinpurses, in the empty spaces in their packs, and in their waterskins.

"We will return to Eloesus," said Theron. "The gods have not smiled on us… but we will find our own fate. Our country will burn."

OUTSIDE THE CITY OF NISSOS

Seven-and-one-half fingers of wood… eight and one-sixth spoons of mercury… quicklime weighing two Eloesian pounds… coal weighing five Eloesian pounds…

Against all odds, against all which Rogon expected, he had found what he needed to make quickfire. In a mortal and pestle he had the alchemical ingredients ground… Then he laid it on the wood, in the bucket of a catapult.

His men had begun to believe they were losing the battle. Yet even in the face of death, they had faith in Rogon. They had faith because he faced death alongside them; he did not ask any more of them than he did of himself. That was the true key to leadership, and to all battles. If he ever asked his soldiers to do something he would not do, they would see right through him.

If he mixed all these ingredients poorly, it would all fail. Yet, with a silent prayer, he took a burning torch and cast it upon the wood like an offering to the gods.

The quickfire burst into blazing light. It was just like he remembered. The fire crackled like bubbling liquid as it emitted a dark black smoke.

Rogon gave the signal, and the catapult flung the nascent quickfire.

The quickfire had consumed the wood, but as it flew through the air the burning, sticky fire continued to adhere. Like a boulder it remained together, launched from the catapult. The fire shifted and twisted as it hurtled through the air and then hit the city gate in a splash.

The wood of the gate burst into flame and within seconds every bit of it was burning. A caustic black smoke billowed out as the fire ate through every last board and plank.

Rogon's men cheered. With renewed vigor the archers shot arrows at the defenders on the walls.

Rogon fought against overconfidence, but he knew in his heart the victory was won. They would have Nissos. They would have it all for themselves.

BRECKONASIA

Laughing, Pygmalia danced out of the city gate with four hundred liberated women behind her. She took a sip of her wine bottle. Cheap wine was all she could purchase under the nose of her husband, but it would work just as well. The less he knew, the better.

With so many women liberated, dancing out of the city gate and laughing loudly, it was impossible to hide. Their husbands had found out, but too late; they could not stop their wives from donning their masks and joining the Breckonalian debauches.

Out into the cool of the Thenoan night she danced. Her friend Demokrita grabbed her hands and they danced together, twisting and turning, laughing and smiling. Was there anything better than liberation? Was there anything better than being a Breckonal?

On a hill, their high priest stood, the one who had led them away from the slavery of logic and common sense and into the freedom of pure emotion. Even in the moonlight, Pygmalia could see he was not alone. Five other shapes, five other silhouettes, could be made out—and she could distinguish the horns and the beards, the hairy goat legs. These were satyrs.

A strange pang of indecision wriggled in Pygmalia's gut—a rare assault of fear and logic, an attack of inhibition. The priest of Brecko—wearing his goat-skin headdress—fixed his gleaming eyes on Pygmalia.

"The Hoofed God has visited you," said the priest.

Like a floodgate, the memories of last night's dream returned to Pygmalia. Tossing and turning in her bed, she had been assailed with a vision, of the goat-footed Brecko, riding on his panther. "I choose you," he had said, "to achieve true passion."

A satyr bounded up to Pygmalia.

The worm of worry, twisting in her stomach, blossomed into full panic. The satyr grabbed Pygmalia's hands; his skin was rough and callused.

Under her breath, Pygmalia whispered what had been taught. "*Nothing matters, only this emotion, this passion—only this moment, not the future, not the past.*"

The satyr's cheeks were red, his eyes hot with lust. She saw—to her panic—the part of him which had grown stiff.

Can I do it? There was nothing she wanted to do less.

The satyr's hands tightened their grip greedily. With his hoofed legs he tried to lead her away. He wanted to possess her.

She resisted only a moment. Louder, she said, "Nothing matters, only this emotion, this passion—only this moment, not the future, not the past!"

Her sisters, the liberated women of Thénai, cheered as she was led away to achieve true Breckonasia.

The panic and inhibition had left her; gleefully she went away with her new lover. From now until the end of her days, there would be no reason or logic, only the present, only the moment, only passion and fear and fury and thirst and hunger and lust.

CITY SQUARE, THÉNAI

Third Night was two weeks away.

Why had the words of the priestess affected Hyron so?

There is one coming who will claim his birthright. You must prepare the temple for him. Drive out the priests of Tyros… re-consecrate it on Third Night.

Perhaps the idle words of the priestess affected him, now, because everything was falling apart. The mad, drunk king of the Isteroi refused to do his duty; all tasks of administration had fallen on Hyron, and the Thenoan League was coming apart at the seams.

They had lost the City of Nissos to the Kersican League; war had been declared, war which the Thenoan League could scarce afford to bear. Out of the ashes of defeat, the Dark Captain—the one named Rogon—had risen again. Theron, hero of the Southron War, was gone, executed after the deceit of the Kersican League.

Who was he to appease the gods? Who was he to re-dedicate the temple when all was lost? Why would he honor the holy gods when they had abandoned him? Why would he do anything at all, except try to preserve his life?

They had a captive, now, an ambassador named Gaia. They kept her not in the grim city prison, but under house arrest. She was a pawn in Hyron's hand; but how could he play this pawn? How could he use her best, and sue for peace?

He had come to the City Square of Thénai, blending in with its merchants and traders, in a search for inspiration. But instead, his despair had only increased. The black spot on his soul had tripled in size. *There is nothing I can do to save our city… nothing at all.*

HOUSE OF THE FROGS, NORTH THÉNAI

In a room, they had kept Gaia. As a high profile captive from whom they hoped to extract a ransom, they had given her a clean room with a bed, and a daily allotment of bread and wine. How different it was from the way they'd treated Theron. The bread was fresh and the wine was of acceptable quality. They had given Theron moldy rations and foul water, all in an attempt to break him. He had at last given up the code, but the Hymnos Device as a whole had failed.

The embarrassment of that moment still stung. But like all other things, she vowed to make the best of it. She would achieve victory, somehow. She had become Korthos' first female ambassador through optimism, confidence, and faith in her abilities.

After she regained her freedom, she would find a way to make things right. She was sure that Rogon failed, that he had lost Nissos; she would regain it. She had failed to resurrect the Hymnos Device; she would find a way to rebuild it.

A tear streaked her cheek. For the first time in her life, she began to sob.

Who was she kidding? She had failed in her endeavors, and had failed badly. There was no going back to the way things were. Everyone in the Assembly back home had witnessed her failure: the Hymnos Device, and now the loss of Nissos.

I will be lucky if they send three thalon *for a ransom.*

Gingerly, she wiped the tears from her eyes. She had to calm herself. She took in deep breaths and stretched her legs, then her arms. Then she got up and knocked on the door.

A guard opened it from the outside.

"I am the Ambassador of Korthos. I demand to speak to your leader… to the archon."

The guard snarled some curse and shut the door. This time, he locked it.

Gaia uttered a curse of her own.

Against the wall, there were two iron-barred windows which just barely let in light. Gaia grabbed her bed and pulled it to face the windows. She climbed onto the mattress and, stretching her legs, managed to peek through to the city below.

The streets below the house—apparently once composed of dirt—were being dug out; workers were pouring gravel in the trench. On the far end of the street, others were fitting white pavestones together. On several of the red-roofed houses below, workers were painting the walls in vivid whites and yellows; on one house, Gaia could make out a worker laying tiles on a roof which had been thatch.

The money pouring into the Thenoan League's treasury at Choros had made the city wealthy beyond the estimations of Gaia's colleagues. War would be costly; the power of the Thenoan League and the Kersican League were roughly equal—according to Gaia's probably overly-sunny estimation.

We need something to put us over the edge. We need help from afar… or an Old Dominion artifact.

Rogon may have survived his certain loss in Nissos. He had allies in the south who could help.

SIREN SQUARE, CITY OF NISSOS

Rogon had never been one for mercy.

The bodies of the dead were strewn all around the City of Nissos, both hoplite and common citizen. The effeminate young man who called himself the prince was bound in manacles—where once slaves had been kept in Siren Square, now the city's ruler was on display.

Rogon knew the dangers in leaving these bodies in the open. The flesh flies would lay their eggs in the corpses and then— when hatched—bite and sting his men. He had seen the rashes and disfigurements of the flesh flies back home. After his old friend Yusor was bitten all over the face, his left eye had turned to milky-white goop, and in the other he was half blind.

But for now, the bodies would lie in the city square, instilling terror in whoever watched. The once-pristine white stone was smeared with blood. The blood of both free and slave had been shed; Rogon had shown no partiality.

Rogon walked up to the young prince. He had been stripped to his underclothes, revealing a slight and scrawny physique. This soft young man had earned Rogon's hatred. Eloesians were cowards and pederasts; this "Alexis" proved it.

He wondered whether he should kill him now. Rogon's advisors had said "Alexis will fetch three *talents* in ransom." But out of the treasury of the Narcissi, Rogon had already seized in excess of five *talents* in gold bars and silver coins. What was three *talents* compared to making an example of this weakling prince?

"What do you want?" Even stripped to his underclothes, tied to rusty manacles, this Alexis ventured an impudent tone. Even at risk of death, Rogon was beneath him.

Rogon wondered if he could sever Alexis' head in one blow. It was worth a try.

But Rogon had learned to trust his advisors. Alexis would keep his life, for now.

The Thenoan navy was blockading the port, letting no food or wine in, nor ships out. Sooner or later, they believed, Rogon and his men would starve.

Viewing the spectacle from the port, Rogon supposed they were probably right. The army had devoured much of the food in the Nissian granary.

Rogon signaled his men to prepare a ship.

Hours later, Rogon himself set sail, despite the danger. He was alone.

The admiral of the squadron met Rogon aboard the flagship. He was dressed in Thenoan blues, wearing a dark blue sash over his tunic which gleamed with medals and service stars. "What do you want?" He had observed the protocol, refusing to hurt Rogon, but his tone was sneering.

"I have come to make you an offer," Rogon said.

The admiral glared, but in addition to pederasts and cowards, Eloesians were lovers of money.

"If you will abandon your post, I will give you one *talent* in gold and silver, and an equal amount distributed to your men."

The admiral scoffed. "I think you should leave, southron. I will not make deals with the Dark Captain."

Rogon couldn't believe it. Still, he maintained his calm. "I will give you ten *talents* in gold bars…"

"No amount of money can cause me to betray my city," the

admiral answered. "I will count down from ten… and if you are not gone, I'll have you executed on the spot."

Rogon cursed. He left the deck hurriedly and returned to his vessel. As he rowed back to shore, with failure weighing heavy on him, he made a vow to succeed despite the danger. He would see all the ships burn; he would see all the sailors sent to a watery grave.

This he vowed, in the name of Athra, god of fire, his lord.

THE SHORE, OUTSIDE THENOA

Ten Days Later…

Sopping wet, Theron at last set his feet on land. He had lost sight of Khloë after the wreck. His ship had been waylaid; pirates had attacked them and set their ship afire. Those pirates had been women, but not amazons.

He hoped in the goddess's name, Amara, that Khloë found her way to shore. Their bond had grown so strong, it would be like losing a piece of him. Khloë had stood up for him where no Eloesian ever had.

Now, if Theron could do as he hoped and burn Eloesus to the ground, it would only be with Khloë's help.

~

The rocky shoals here along the Thenoan inlet was overrun by cypresses and scrub brush. No people lived here, around this poor soil. Water was scarce, and civilization was impossibly far away. Theron had no food; Khloë alone knew how to hunt. But more than that, if Khloë was lost, Theron simply couldn't go on. Through all the trials of betrayal and abandonment, Khloë was the only one who had stood by him. Daphnë was just like the Eloesians; she had betrayed him, too, by dying.

He still remembered her bloodless corpse, her body stripped nude, punctured by knife wounds. A robber had taken her. How could someone kill such a good woman, only for gold?

In the weeks leading up to her death, she had spoken often of how she missed her homeland. It was a hard adjustment, seeing a country where the men ruled over the women. "Tigris would be lovely, this time of year," she said one winter night.

In all that time, she had never complained of her new, hard life without servants or slaves. All she had wanted was Theron.

And then she had died, leaving him a broken man.

THE THENOAN INLET

Khloë was splashing hopelessly through the water, through the churning waves of the sea. The sea was part of the amazonian life; yet Khloë had never been a good swimmer. As a young girl, when the ways of war were taught to her, she had shown little interest in swimming. Where the other girls would socialize by diving through the waves, Khloë had retreated to the shade of a palm tree and sharpened her sword. There, her thoughts would run wild. There, her dreams were formed: *I will see the world. I will go to the human realm.*

Struggling against the waves with their towering pinnacles, Khloë swam east, away from the waning sun. Was she a hundred miles out to sea? Two hundred? Gods only knew.

The gods could not help her. She was going to die.

~

Exhaustion began to set in as the sun dipped below the waters.

Her mouth tasted of saltwater. Lethargy had replaced panic; she had begun to welcome the idea of her watery tomb, beneath the sea.

The fading light reflected against a dark shape—a three-sailed ship, gliding through the waters.

In a frenzy, her will to live returned, and she swam as fast as she could towards it.

But the winds were carrying it away. She was too slow. And now all her energy was gone. *How long until I give up? How long until I sink into the tomb prepared for me?*

~

Her head was bobbing underwater. Her strength was fading. She swallowed a mouthful of ocean water and spat it out in a coughing fit. She wasn't trying anymore, just floating amid the waves.

The last fading glimpse of sunlight illuminated the wreckage of the ship she had left behind.

In all these hours of supposed swimming, she had crossed no distance at all.

She swam toward the ship's husk, hoping for a miracle.

~

The ship's deck had disintegrated. Her sabers had fallen to the briny deeps. She grabbed onto a blackened board and, for the first time in a day, relaxed.

She awoke in the middle of the night with the board having disintegrated underneath her. The waves had carried her far from the wreckage of the ship, but where was she now.

She spat out salty ocean water. She had no energy left. She began to dip and bob underwater again.

Her strength gave out, and she slipped beneath the ocean's waves.

When she came to, she was on the deck of a ship, and it was morning.

Sailors were scurrying across the deck, as sailors did. The sunlight was burning on Khloë. She was wearing nothing but her smock. Her sabers and her armor were gone, as was all the gold she had stolen from the Khazidean temple.

In her safety, she—for the first time—pondered the strangeness of what had occurred. A ship-full of women, not amazons, had waylaid them and thrown them overboard.

These Eloesian women had overpowered them by sheer force of numbers. They had surprised Theron and sent him hurtling over the deck.

Khloë had slashed one assailant to death before the team—two-hundred strong—charged and threw her overboard as well.

Then they had lit the ship on fire until a column of smoke covered the sky. They departed from where they had come.

Who were these people? Eloesian women tended not to be pirates. They had a singular purpose: to kill Theron and Khloë. They also had knowledge of where Theron and Khloë were.

Perhaps, Khloë would never know their identity.

Dizzy and starving, Khloë shouted to any sailor who would hear her: "Where am I?"

"You are aboard *The Gold Trident*," one answered. "It is the second hour, and we are carrying a load of perfumes to the great city of Thénai."

Where was Theron? She knew, in her heart, he could not be dead.

SIREN SQUARE, CITY OF NISSOS

"Go," said Rogon to the group of soldiers who had gathered before him, "Find everything we needed for quickfire— quicklime, mercury, and coal—and collect ten times more."

As they ran off, Rogon turned to face the harbor. The blockade had held firm. Rogon had gained respect for these Thenoans, who would not stray from their loyalty even in the face of a bribe. But they would fail. He would make it so.

~

Rogon had serious doubts the men would find what they were looking for. But it was worth the effort.

He ordered Prince Alexis un-shackled. "Give him food," he told one of his officers. "And comfortable clothing. Let him stay in the palace if he wishes."

But even in the palace, the prince of the Royal Line of Narcissi would not find the same creature comforts he once enjoyed. The bloodshed had reduced the once-great city of Nissos to the size of a village. Slave and free, they had been put to the sword.

Prince Alexis glared at Rogon as the soldiers unchained him. There was hatred in those eyes, enough hatred to melt him.

Once free, Prince Alexis didn't move. He was flexing his hands. "You butchered my people. Gods take your life, and send you to the underworld!" He charged Rogon and leapt upon him.

Rogon fell despite the prince's slight weight. As the prince clawed and scratched and punched him, he tried desperately to throw him off, but there was strength in this Prince Alexis, strength that surprised Rogon—strength born of anger.

In a moment, three swords were plunged into Alexis, and blood spurted from his body. Rogon heaved Alexis off him; weighed down by armor, it took the help of three men to hoist Rogon to his feet.

A flesh fly buzzed by his ear. It was time to remove the dead.

~

They laid the frail body of Prince Alexis on the top of the body pile. His men estimated five-thousand dead in the city, and another ten-thousand remaining alive.

On a bed of wood, the mass of bodies had been laid. The rotting corpses were higher than Nissos' temple. Rogon gave the signal and torches were thrown upon the oiled wood.

Then Rogon left into the night, hoping to avoid the stench.

~

He was not long out of the city gates when the battalion he had sent out returned. They were empty handed.

Elliadēs, the leader, had the look of fear in his eyes. "Rogon," he said, "we could not search the villages for what you needed. The whole island is in rebellion! They have all taken up swords, the women and children too…"

Rogon realized out of the thirty he sent, only ten were here. No doubt they had been killed by the villagers, who had heard of Nissos' slaughter.

But Elliadēs was not done. "A Thenoan army has landed," he said. "I don't know how many. They are pouring out of the ships. We must fortify Nissos… we must repair the walls or else we're done for…"

And we are done for, a lesser captain would say. But Rogon was better than that. Without a trace of fear in his voice, he said, "We must come together. We will prevail…"

THÉNAI HARBOR

When Khloë departed the merchant ship, she pressed the captain Nikator to finally return home and visit his family in Adamantis. She encouraged the first mate Giton to pursue his one true love Soteria. She wished the best of luck to the surgeon Argenton, whose wife was suffering from a years-long illness. She bade farewell to all the boatswains and cabin boys by name.

In just two days of sailing, she had gotten to know every crew member aboard *The Gold Trident*, and she was remorseful as she left.

But the departure of the crew soon became the least of her sorrows. Theron was a good swimmer, and stronger—physically and mentally—than anyone she had ever known. She had a feeling deep in her heart that he was alive; but could her hopes betray her? Perhaps the mighty sea had claimed him.

At the thought, her eyes watered. He had become a dearer friend to her than anyone else in this world.

~

In the City Square, crowded with market stalls, there was a statue of a man whom Khloë did not recognize. He was fat and bearded, wearing a crown, and bearing in his marble hands a sword.

The City Square's beauty dwarfed any in Korthos. The tile of the square was in bright green, red, and blue patterns against a white background. It was kept clean and layered with something like wax.

Khloë was penniless; she had lost everything. How long before she starved?

She was not a Thenoan citizen. No one would take care of her. Perhaps she would become a beggar, surviving on the scraps of food Thenoans tossed away. She belonged to no one.

Would her sisters take her back if she returned to the old world, if she disappeared once more into the place she had left behind? Amazonia had become a gloomy place. As the amazon world fell back into the shadows, her people—the huntresses in the wood, the warriors, the queens, the shepherdesses, the Solarine— had become shades of what they once were.

Perhaps that is where Khloë belonged. These humans did not respect amazons. Even if Khloë were granted citizenship in Thénai, like she had in Korthos, she would never be considered one of them.

If she climbed to the top of the High City, towering above her, and laid an offering before its gleaming white temple, if she cut her hands and spilled her blood on the altar, if she swore to honor Thénai's gods and pledge her utmost to the city's name, still she would find no acceptance.

She wandered City Square aimlessly. She became convinced Theron was dead. Tomorrow, she would return to the old world she had left behind. Along with Amazonia itself, she would retreat into the shadows. The Eloesians would never hear from her again.

"Two sabers, finely crafted!" shouted a merchant who had set up a stall in City Square. "Two sabers sharp and fine! Sharp enough to slice a rock! Twenty *doukon* for both!"

Khloë did not know why she was drawn to this merchant or what attracted her about his voice. Perhaps it was what he said.

She approached the stall and there, in his hands, were Khloë's own sabers. They had been pilfered from the wreck.

Khloë's first instinct was to strike the man; to knock him in the ground and savage him with blows.

That is what she would have done, months ago, before she met Theron, before he had taught her the wisdom of planning and forethought. Instead, she restrained her hands, she resisted her violent urges. She asked him, calmly, "Where did you get those sabers?"

"I purchased them from a smith of Nissos," he said. "He crafted them from the metal of a fallen star."

"You lie!" Khloë shouted and the urge to savage this man grew tenfold. But instead, she kept her calm. "Those sabers were stolen from me. I purchased them years ago. I was attacked in the sea. You are selling stolen goods."

The merchant turned pale.

"I will tell the magistrate you're selling stolen goods," Khloë said. "Tell me where you got them!"

"A woman sold them to me," the merchant answered. "A group of other women were with her. They had their hair covered. They were dressed in blue. They were Maids of the Mount of Prophecy. They were the women of the Oracle."

Khloë couldn't believe it. Why would the Oracle attack Theron? What would Mount Hylea have against Theron, the hero of the Southron War?

"They sold them to me for ten *doukon*. Do you have the money to repay me?"

"No."

The merchant frowned. "Here you go…" He handed over the sabers.

Stunned, Khloë stood there a moment, lost in thought, wondering why on earth the Oracle on the holy Mount would turn against Theron. How could she attack the one she had once called?

She left without answers. She was better armed, and in possession of her most valued belongings; but she had lost her friend. She would wait for him here. If he was alive, surely he would return to his home. If he went anywhere, he would go to Thénai.

THE BATTLEMENTS, NISSOS

Ten Days Later...

Under constant assault, Rogon's men had stood firm. The armies of Thénai had failed to breach the wall. But food was running low, and the remaining citizens of Nissos were growing restless. Rogon's men were growing weary, and day by day their number was dwindling. Two hundred had died since the assault began; and Rogon, fighting alongside his men, had witnessed the bloodshed.

A bright flash illuminated the dark of the night. Rogon turned back to look. Pausing from the battle, he could see the inky-black sea of the harbor reflecting a bright shade of red.

The Thenoan flagship had caught fire. More blazes had started; in the light of the flame, Rogon could see a fleet of a hundred warships approaching the Thenoan position. These warships bore the flag of the Kersican League. They used the weapons of the Korthians: a weapon Rogon had helped develop, a fast-burning fire.

The tide had changed.

All doubt was removed. Nissos was theirs. Victory was won.

~

Reinforcements poured in all through the night. Another fifteen thousand Kersepolan hoplites were added to Rogon's number.

By morning, the Thenoan force had retreated far beyond

the walls to take shelter in the outlying villages.

In Siren Square, Rogon met the leader of the Kersepolans: King Helion himself.

"We heard you were in trouble." He laughed. The black-bearded King of Kersepoli wore a breastplate forged into the shape of muscles and a cape of blood-red crimson. "You were outnumbered but I knew you would hold out. There is no better Strategos than you, Rogon, in all of Eloesus and in the Southern World."

Rogon smiled. He did not care for empty praise. It was the victory that filled him with joy.

The City of Nissos would rebuild… their population would come to enjoy the benefits of the Kersican League. Their hatred for Rogon would endure; but they would never rebel.

"Gaia has been taken," King Helion said. "She is captive in Thénai. They are demanding five *talents* for her return."

"Let her rot in chains," Rogon said. "I don't care for her at all."

HOUSE OF THE FROGS, NORTH THÉNAI

Gaia wept, as she had so often done these past few nights. She had entered the House of Frogs with confidence; now, as weeks passed, she had become convinced no one would pay her ransom.

What worth was she to her beloved city, anyway? She had always thought of herself as a distinguished citizen, as a valued member of Korthos. Now, she wasn't so sure. What value did she bring to her city? What did she offer? Certainly nothing worth a five-*talent* ransom.

She was not a praying woman. There was no proof for the gods or goddesses, no reason to believe in their existence. The naturalist philosophers had it right; there was nothing except the world around them.

The kindness of the Thenoans struck her deeper than anything. Each day, they offered her fresh hot bread and a cup of watered-down wine.

She had delighted in tormenting Thénai's chief citizen, Theron. She had served him moldy bread and water of questionable sanitation. The good treatment she was afforded seemed only a further dagger in the heart.

And so, she was weeping silently, hoping desperately for a way out. But she remained in the House of Frogs; and what came next, she did not know. Only one thing was certain: the ransom would never be paid. She would never return to Korthos alive.

THENOAN WILDERNESS

The sun was baking down on Theron; amid the waterless scrub grass he had grown delirious. He had followed the shore south, but failed to find civilization.

There were cypresses clinging to mountainous hills. There were sparrows and eagles scouring the land for prey. Theron had feasted on what little food he could find: berries and nuts, small scraps of meat. He had cooked the carcass of a bird on a fire and choked down the rancid meat. Yet hunger, for all these days, had been constantly present. There was no escaping his weakening body, his empty stomach—and the burning hot sun.

~

On the eleventh day since the wreck, as he staggered on, he came to a series of grassy hills. In the distance there were sheep, recently shorn, grazing on a golden hill. They were led by a shepherd.

In a frenzy—whether in panic or excitement—Theron took off at a sprint.

The heat overwhelmed him and he blacked out, falling to the ground.

When he woke up the sheep had surrounded him, and the shepherd had put a waterskin to Theron's mouth.

He gulped down the clear, clean liquid like it was the finest bottle of wine. He had not drunk such clean water for weeks. Even aboard the ship with Khloë, the sailors had not fed them well. The watered down wine had tasted of sea salt. The bread was so stale even Khloë had complained.

Khloë. What had happened to her? Theron had to move on.

That night, the shepherd gathered sticks and firewood. He slit the throat of a ram and dressed the animal over the course of hours. The skin, he set out to dry.

Theron had learned this shepherd's name was Dion, and that he had been born in the city of Thénai. His father had been a citizen of some note, and had once led ceremonies during Third Night.

"I saw the cruelty of the city," Dion said as the haunches of meat roasted, glistening with fat as they were spun around on the fire. "I saw the ambition of the politicians and the callous treatment of the poor. I knew my family was just one false step from becoming a beggar… and so I left. I left it all behind. I will never go back."

Theron's stomach growled. Even in Khazidea, he had not seen such a feast. This food would not only tide him over, it would fill him with strength. It would stick to his ribs; he would sleep well tonight.

"Sheep don't backstab," said Dion. "Sheep don't turn on me… even when I take one of them to the slaughter." Dion's eyes glinted in the fire. "Where are you going?"

Was there any point in a lie? "I am going to Thénai," he answered. "I'm going to burn it to the ground… by myself, if I have to."

Dion laughed. "The leg is done." He pried the haunch of lamb off the fire spit. He tossed the scalding hot morsel to Theron.

Theron never remembered any food tasting this good. Its fatty sinews, its meat and gristle, all of it he devoured like an animal.

He ate every bit of it—fat, meat, cartilage. He chewed around the bone until there was nothing left.

And there was more coming. Was this shepherd sent by the gods—or by Theron's patron, the Oracle? It certainly seemed that way.

Theron ate until his stomach felt like bursting, until the thought of one more haunch sickened him. He ate until it hurt. "Thank you, Dion," he said.

Dion smiled. "Now it's time for you to rest."

That morning, Dion gave Theron a satchel of meat which had been salted and preserved. He invoked the blessing of the god Brecko, who—in addition to wine, pleasure and emotion—was the patron of shepherds and country folk.

Then he handed him a heavy club.

This club was weighted with lead like the one Theron had purchased in Khazidea, but it was much finer, crafted of oak, sanded and polished. It was heavier and would pack a much larger punch.

"If you are going to burn down Thénai and kill all those wicked city folk, you'd best take this," Dion said and smiled. "I had it whittled and weighted years ago. I call it the titan's fist. It has killed many wolves."

"*Titan's Fist*," Theron repeated. "Dion, you have given me more than I could possibly deserve. I can't pay you back."

"You can pay me back by burning Thénai to the ground." Dion laughed. "Good luck, Theron... may Brecko favor your undertakings."

~

And so, Theron set out. Late in the day, according to Dion's directions, he found the road. It would take him directly to the Lion's Gate, to Thénai, the city which had become his enemy.

CITY SQUARE, THÉNAI

The Assembly had been abolished and Hyron would forever mourn the deaths of his friends. Now, as *de facto* archon while King Kunar spent his days drinking, he had hoped to at least escape some of the bureaucratic bickering and outrageous proposals that had annoyed him in the past.

But a man had approached him as Hyron was crossing City Square, a man who had pestered him before.

"Hyron! Your Honor! A word!"

Hyron knew what this was about. His name was Polyarchēs, and he lived on Fishers Street—as he had said many times before.

"My wife has joined the Cult of Brecko!"

This was new. Last time, this man had complained of how far he had to walk to the well.

"I can't help but wonder!" he said, hysterical as always. "I hear these 'Breckonals' bed satyrs…"

Hyron almost laughed. "Well, when your next child comes out hairy and with horns, you can get a divorce!"

The complainer gasped. "You aren't taking it seriously! There are already five women on Fishers Street who joined the cult! It's an epidemic!"

"The only epidemics I deal with are dysentery and the plague." He walked past the stunned complainer. Hyron's authority did not permit him to intervene… although he understood the shame of being a satyr's cuckold.

Hyron turned his eyes to the High City. A towering rock edifice, it stretched high above all the buildings. The marble temple once belonged to Amara, virgin queen of war. Now the priests of Tyros worshiped there—honoring her brother. Surely if the goddess existed—as the common people believed—she would not mind the Eloesians honoring her brother.

He would not do as the liar priestess of Amara wanted. He had trusted the goddess, in vain, before. He would not drive out the priests of Tyros. There was "one coming," they said—but whoever came could deal with the sacrilege.

On Third Night, the goddess would have to find her own way to solve problems. On Third Night, Tyros would be honored. Who cared which powerless figment of imagination was revered?

GREAT ARCTOS ROAD, OUTSIDE THÉNAI

With Third Night three days away, Theron questioned whether he should enter the city. He had no misconceptions about the danger he might be in. Nor did he have any plans once he entered Thénai; only trust in his strength and in the passion of his anger—and in the strength of his club, *Titan's Fist*. The population of Thénai swelled on Third Night as shepherds and country people entered with their sacrifices. The market of Thénai would be crammed with people. The heat would be even more unbearable in the city. And he had no plan.

A signpost read:

THÉNAI: FOUR MILES

A black bird was perched upon the signpost.

The road was packed with people. Suddenly, the heat got to Theron. The weight of the lionskin seemed unbearable. In the distance were mountains. He recognized this place, filled with cypresses, which was anciently called Stygia. He could see the laurel trees, cypresses and pines of a great forest—the ancient and venerable Wood of Gygēs, where Phillipidēs received wisdom hundreds of years ago.

He could sense the tension which filled Thénai. He could sense it in the air, in the conversations of passersby.

Inexplicably, Theron turned off the road and headed into the land once called Stygia, where few now tread.

THENOAN WILDERNESS

Among the cypresses and holm oaks, the sun blazed down and drained the land of all its water. The sky was blue and cloudless. Summer refused to relinquish its grip.

Crickets and frogs were chirping; birds flitted from tree to tree, and Theron stumbled into the wilderness, seeking something, he did not know what.

~

When the day waned, Theron was deep within the wilderness, a land of mixed grassland and scrub forest. He came to a crater lake which had dried out. The dry earth had formed a deep pit which had calcified and turned to rock. This was the ancient stygian lake, where a creature of heaven had fallen like a shooting star, and imbued the water with power.

Pebbles scattered in the distance. Theron was not alone.

He took up his club, *Titan's Fist,* confident that he could destroy anything, man or beast.

The mountainous land around him was shrouded in trees. There was no way of seeing anything. There was no way of knowing where the disturbance had begun.

Night was falling soon, but Theron feared nothing and no one. He had slain the Carceran Lion; was there anything he could not lay low?

Looking at the crater of bright white rock, he recalled the stories of Phillipidēs which his friend Phaido—gods rest his soul—had told. In Stygia he had learned the art of war; he had been tested, and he had failed. It was here, in this ancient land, where he had become a hero.

Pebbles scrambled again.

It came from the woods surrounding the lake, from the deep depths of the pines and holm oaks. Instantly, Theron chased after it. He would kill whatever pursued him, and he would lay it low. He would have its head, just as he had the Carceran Lion. Even the mighty titan stood no chance against him.

Running at full speed, a dark shadow appeared ahead of him. He made out the sight of hooves as it darted away. Its speed did not matter. He would find a way to bring it down. He grabbed a rock from the forest floor and broke into a sprint, faster than he had ever run before.

The woods soon opened up—and Theron almost fell. His heart rose up in his chest; he gasped in panic as he almost teetered off a sheer cliff face. The drop would have killed him—even Theron, who slew the Carceran Lion.

He turned and caught sight of the silhouette again. Again he sprinted forward, seeing a human-like shadow. Soon even the shadow disappeared, leading Theron higher and higher.

Up the mountain Theron was drawn. Three times he threw a stone at his pursuer; three times he missed. He kept running, exerting himself to his limit, as the sunlight began to dwindle. With a stone in his left hand and his club in his right, he continued the naked pursuit. He would slay this creature, whatever it was. He would not rest until it was dead.

Panting and dripping with sweat, he had reached the top of the hill, and he could see the white rock of the stygian crater far below. The creature which had haunted him was nowhere in sight. From this height he could make out snowcapped mountains, and the sea—even the city of Thénai far away, a small inky blot in the distance.

Had the creature retreated?

An arrow struck him in the shoulder. Shocked he stumbled back as he began to bleed.

Out of the woods emerged a creature with a humanoid torso above the waist, and a horse-like body below.

His eyes were bright blue. His ears came to characteristic points. His hair was silver and his skin showed signs of wrinkles.

This was a centaur. The centaurs had died out in the time of Phillipidēs—or so everyone thought.

"Who are you?" Theron said. He ripped the arrow from his shoulder, and his eyes teared up at the pain.

"My name is Aigon."

Theron recognized that name, though he did not know from where. He had ripped out the arrow but the steel head remained within. If he did not find help, he would surely die.

"You are in danger," said Aigon.

A drowsiness had begun to set in. Theron stumbled forward. The arrow had been poisoned.

"You do not trust me," said Aigon. "You are being followed. I had no choice but to draw you away. There are forces working against you, forces you cannot fathom."

Aigon galloped forward as Theron began to fall. He scooped Theron in his giant hands as black circles formed around his vision.

"These dark forces came against Phillipidēs, too," Aigon said as Theron fell asleep.

HOUSE OF THE FROGS, NORTH THÉNAI

Gaia was in one of her weeping fits when the door opened. Quickly she wiped her eyes, but she could not hide their redness. Her captors knew her weakness. Her captors knew the depth of her sorrows, and of her despair. They knew she had become frail.

The leader of Thénai, Hyron, had come.

"You are being released," he said. "We are providing an escort back to Korthos."

"They paid the ransom?" she said, and in an instant her grief vanished like water in the desert sun.

"No," said Hyron. "The ransom was refused. But King Kunar is merciful. He cannot bear to kill a woman, especially not on Third Night. Consider it piety. Consider it grace by the gods."

The grief returned, weighing her down like a millstone, tied around her neck. Was it better to kill her than return in disgrace? How could she face her old life in Korthos, when she had been brought so low?

She could hear the demiarchs in the Korthian Assembly now: *"We refused to pay your ransom. Why are you here?"*

From the heights of power, she had been squashed to the stature of an ant. When she returned to Korthos, would she fling herself off the High City? *No, I will find some way to endure…*

HEAVEN'S SQUARE, KORTHOS

On carts, Rogon's soldiers had laid the rich loot of plunder. Behind him in the procession were priceless paintings, gold ornaments and marble statues, piles of gold necklaces, rings and amulets; and statues of gold with diamond eyes—all the wealth of Nissos on display.

Rogon rode on a white horse, the symbol of a conqueror; and he had been given a cloak of crimson, representing the blood of his enemies. He had little doubt he'd be put in control of the entire Kersican League; and from there, he could finish the work he had begun.

The cheering crowds lining Heaven's Square masked the hatred growing across the land. Already he had earned hateful monikers: "The Dark Captain," "The King-Killer," "The Butcher of Nissos." But to be great, and to earn victory, all that came with enmity and hatred.

It did not matter. He had succeeded. He had carved a path before him, and soon all of Eloesus would be in his control.

CITY SQUARE, KORTHOS

Everyone would eat well tonight, feasting on the fattened calves of Third Night's sacrifices. But Khloë's mind was somewhere altogether different. She had become convinced that Theron—if he survived—was in terrible danger. She had to find him. She had to rescue him. But how?

Dark clouds were forming over Eloesus, evil forces which Khloë did not understand. She had to find him; she had to bring Theron home, before it was too late. She—feeble Khloë—had to rescue Theron before he was found. She, feeble Khloë, had to save Theron, the hero of the Southron War.

GAMMAHEDRON

Days Later…

In a field outside of Korthos, Gaia once again risked everything.

Another machine had been assembled, another attempt to complete the Hymnos Device.

When she had entered the gates of Korthos in the despair, the inventor locked in the library had declared to her, "I have found it!" Buried in the depths of Korthos' library he had found blueprints which exactly matched the Hymnos device. "It is not a *Mekahedron*," he had exclaimed, "but a *Gammahedron!*"

What was a Gammahedron, she had asked him. And he did not know—only that the plans he found were titled "Gammahedron."

The device looked similar, with a giant drill and a large body of gears and wheels. But it was much larger than the so-called *Mekahedron*.

Coolly, Gaia stood in front of the device. She set out the code which Theron had given her:

⅃⊦⊦⊣⊣

Then, knowing her life was at risk if even the slightest bit of the machine was improperly crafted, she pulled the lever.

The engine blazed into life. There was a thunderous, booming sound which became deafening. The skeptical crowd covered their ears. The drill at the front sizzled with lightning; a beam began to form, bright and red, and blasted forward.

The dummy wall had been erected to show its destructive power; but the beam stopped inches short of the wall.

Instead, a sheet of bright light formed, and the very fabric of reality seemed to taper away.

The sheet of light began to fade, forming a border; and it became a window into a world of fire—a world whose sky was yellow as sulfur.

The Hymnos Device was not an engine of war. It was not a destructive force.

It was a portal!

CONTINUED IN BOOK 5, 'WRATH OF THE DEMIURGE'

GLOSSARY

Thalos: A small silver coin, worth one-fourth a *doukos.* Plural *thalon.*

Doukos: The standard silver coin across Eloesus. It takes many forms but generally has the city's patron god cast onto the front and the victory laurel wreath on the back. Plural *doukon.* One *doukos* is about the daily wage of a skilled laborer.

Oros: A gold coin, worth fifty *doukon.* Plural *orhon.*

Talent: A unit of measurement, worth one-thousand *doukon.*

Adamantis: A small island off the coast of Eloesus. Its capital is a city of the same name.

Alabastros: The king of the gods in the Eloesian pantheon. He is revered especially by the Thartans. As king of the gods, he is considered to preside over kingship, leadership, and royalty. He is often depicted as a wise old man. His favored animal is the lion.

Amara: The goddess of motherly love in the Eloesian pantheon. In Thénai and the Amazonian Isles, she is also the goddess of wisdom and battle. Although a mother, she is a virgin. Eloesian legend states she is the daughter of Alabastros and the Earth. Her brother is Tyros, god of war.

Amazonia: A term for amazon lands. Amazonia encompasses the islands of Jogheira, Straiteira, Agathë, Kalormenë and a few smaller islands.

Amazons, the: A race of people living in the coastal islands off the Eloesian shore. Their women are far stronger and—some argue—more intelligent than their men. Though they look similar to humans, amazons and humans cannot breed. The child of an amazon and a human is always stillborn.

Arkadian hills: Hills outside the village of Arkadion in Themuria, believed to be sacred to the god Brecko.

Arkadion: A village, the largest in the wilds of Themuria, called the Bride of the Wilderness. It has recently sworn allegiance to the Thenoan league. The village lies in view of the sacred Mount of Prophecy.

Athra: In Fharese mythology, the god of fire.

Alesis: A port town outside Korthos. It has always served as Korthos' port, but recently the Long Walls were built, connecting it to the city proper.

Algabal: The second largest city in Khazidea, a temple city and a center of wealth.

Blue Desert: The desert west of the Khazan River Delta, named for its proximity to the kingdom of Kheroe, whose heraldic symbol is blue.

Brecko: The god of wine, song, and theater. He is also considered the King of the Satyrs. He is pictured as a fat man with goat legs, accompanied at all times by his pet panther. According to Eloesian legend, he is the son of Tyros, god of war, and Seladora, goddess of nature. His sister is Nix (see below) whom he fears.

Carceros: According to legend, the lowest portion of the underworld: a place of evil chthonic kingdoms and demonic creatures. It is located far beneath the surface of the earth.

Centaur: Creatures whom Eloesians depicted with the lower bodies of horses and the upper bodies of humans. The greatest of the centaurs was named Aigon, who tutored many heroes in ancient days. Aigon was exceptional in his patience and intelligence; centaurs had a reputation for drunkenness and debauchery. Wars between centaur tribes, and wars between the centaurs and the Eloesians, drove them to extinction hundreds of years ago.

Chiton: A knee-length sleeveless shirt, once popular across Eloesus but now restricted to priests and government officials.

Choros: An island eleven miles northwest of Thénai. As the home for the treasury of the Thenoan League, it is heavily fortified and garrisoned with thousands of troops.

Civic gods: The gods considered sacred to a particular city. Tharta favors Alabastros; Korthos, Nix and Arephon; Kersepoli, Tyros lord of war; and Thénai, Amara.

Democrats: In Eloesian parlance, supporters of democracy. They defend giving power to the people, as opposed to monarchists who believe in the divine right of kings.

Dys: A land far west from Eloesus across the sea, on the border of the ocean, little known and little explored. Thartan settlers planted cities along its western and southern coasts: Mageios, Lornadion, and Agathion.

Eastrons: A term used by the Fharese and Khazideans, often derogatively, for Eloesians.

Fharas: A vast empire, by far the strongest power in the world. It is ruled by the King of Kings, who is considered a living god. The word Fharas and Fharese also refers to a certain region and people—the heartland where the empire began.

Fields of Paradise: According to Eloesian religion, a region of heaven where the heroes and certain virtuous mortals go after death.

Firewater: An extremely strong, colorless and harsh alcoholic drink preferred by the amazons.

Gnosor: A general of the ancient world who wrote a book, "On War."

Herodium: In Eloesus, a shrine built specifically for heroes as well as semi-divine demigods. The greatest of the herodiums is in Tharta, honoring Phillipidēs.

High city: A common feature of all Eloesian cities, a towering high ground—natural or man made—which serves as a fortress in times of trouble.

Hordo: The wife of the founder of Thenoan democracy, Ansolon.

Hoplite: The traditional soldier in the Eloesian army. Each hoplite has a helmet and a breastplate, a spear and a shortsword, in addition to an iron-rimmed wooden shield. When fighting, he locks shields with his fellow hoplites, forming an impenetrable wall as long as he holds formation.

Isteros: A region in the north of Eloesus, along the river Ister. The Isteroi speak a dialect of Eloesian but are thought to be outsiders, due to their pallid complexions and frequently red hair.

Juggernaut, the: The largest of amazon warships, designed in the square shape of gold arks but possessing many sails, as well as an on-deck catapult, a ramming device as well as numerous battering rams.

Kersican League: A union of Eloesian city-states with Kersepoli as the head. Megaris and the Ten Cities announced their membership within months of the Southron War's ending; a small handful of other cities in mainland Eloesus also joined.

Korthos: A large city, one of the four greatest in Eloesus. It is ruled by an Assembly, elected by the people, and an archon, elected by the Assembly.

Lion's Gate, the: The main gate of Thénai. Two lions are carved in stone above its giant double doors.

Magi: The priesthood of Fharas. They worship the god of fire, Athra, and revere all flames as sacred. Only youth with magical talent are chosen; they are taught both about the god Athra and also the skill of conjuring and controlling fire. Since magical talent is rare and can be found among the peasantry, becoming a magus is one of the few opportunities for advancement in Fharas's class-based society.

Nissos: A remote island off the coast of Eloesus, the center of the slave trade. It is one of the wealthiest areas in the island region.

The capital of Nissos bears the same name as the island, called the City of Nissos or merely the City. It is ruled by princes of the Narcissi family.

Nix: The goddess of secrets and whispers, her followers call her the Gray Lady or the Queen of Sorcery. She presides over the knowledge of herbs—healing and poisonous—as well as hidden knowledge, wisdom, and the metals iron and silver. She is feared throughout Eloesus, though her name is invoked for protection from the unquiet dead. Korthos was historically the center of her worship. Her favored animals are the owl and the dog. According to Eloesian legend, she is the daughter of Tyros, god of war, and Seladora, goddess of nature. She was hated by her parents and cast out of the household.

Old Dominion, the: A legendary empire which was said to rule the entire world. It was destroyed suddenly, in one night, by fire and ash. Its cities sank into the sea. Though now a distant memory, it is the source of many legends. Its artifacts are scattered throughout Eloesus: engines and technologies of great power, which reinforce the idea of the Old Dominion as a lost "golden age."

Phillipidēs: An Eloesian legendary hero, the son of a Thartan noble who fought in the Megarine War. According to myth, he was given a magic helmet by the goddess Amara which made him invincible to mortal weapons.

Politarch: In the cities of Eloesus, these are the government officials answerable directly to the Assembly. They are charged with certain categories of oversight; thus one politarch might manage the food supply, the other the water. In Korthos and Thénai, they are appointed by the Assembly; in Kersepoli and Tharta they are appointed by kings. Their duties vary from one city to the other.

Qaz Khabar: A temple city of Khazidea, considered the capital of

Qabash (see below).

Qabash: A fertile region in western Khazidea.

Red Desert: The desert east of Khazidea, named for its red rocks and canyons.

Saif: A port city in western Khazidea.

Sarxopoli: An Eloesian colony in mountainous eastern Khazidea.

Slavery: The institution is widespread in Fharas and offers slaves no rights whatsoever; they are viewed as objects or tools, not human beings. In Eloesus, the institution is banned altogether in Thénai and heavily regulated in Korthica and Thartica. Slaves have no rights in Kersepoli.

Southrons: A term for the Fharese, Khazideans, and more generally people from the far south.

Solarine, the: In Amazonia, an order of warriors and magic weavers dedicated to the sun. Only women with magical talent may become Solarine. In addition to serving as religious leaders to the amazons, they have can summon gouts of bright flame—a flame so powerful it disintegrates everything it touches. They wear simple cloth robes and wield giant spiked clubs.

Stygia: An ancient region named for the ruined city-state of Stygidos. A heavenly being was said to have died in a lake nearby, imbuing the waters with its blood.

Ten Cities: A confederation of ten city-states, west from Eloesus across a desert, with Megaris as its head. The Ten Cities take great pride in their half-southron, half-Eloesian identity. They say they form a bridge between Fharese despotism and Eloesian democracy.

Tharta: A great city, considered the chief in Eloesus. It is ruled by a king but has certain limited forms of democracy.

Thénai: A large city, one of the four greatest in Eloesus. It is ruled by an Assembly, elected by the people, and an archon, elected by the Assembly.

Thenoan League: A union of Eloesian city-states with members across the Middle Sea. The headquarters of the League is in Thénai, where the League treasury is located and all League decisions are made.

Third Night: A feast day in summer, celebrating the dedication of the oracle's temple on Mount Hylea. As the holiest day in the Eloesian calendar, the favored gods of each city are honored with religious processions.

Triton: A creature said to live in the depths of the sea, with a humanoid upper body and a lobster-like lower body. Tritons are said to have—instead of hands—large pincers which are strong enough to pierce iron. They are so rarely seen above-water that tritons are often called creatures of myth; yet many sailors would swear on oath to have seen them.

Tyros: The god of war. He is revered in Kersepoli and Isteros; yet he is viewed as never favoring one city over the other, delighting only in battle itself and spilled blood. According to Eloesian legend, he was the son of Alabastros and the Earth. His sister is Amara and his daughter is Nix, whom he hates.

ABOUT THE AUTHOR

Cursed at birth with a wild imagination, Andrew Cooper spent his youth dreaming of worlds more exciting than Earth.

He is a graduate of the Odyssey Writing Workshop. His stories have appeared in Morpheus Tales, Fear and Trembling, Residential Aliens and Mindflights, among others.

CONTACT THE AUTHOR

Visit **www.aj-cooper.com** to sign up for the newsletter and stay up-to-date on new releases.

Find him on Facebook at:

www.facebook.com/AJCooperauthor